# Curvy Girls Can Rule

Ann Maree Craven
Michelle MacQueen

*For everyone who struggles trying to figure out who they are. For the bullied, the outcasts, anyone who only sees imperfections. Growing up is war, high school is a jungle. Just remember, you're not alone.*

# About this book

**Guys aren't supposed to fall for their curvy best friend.**

**They're also not supposed to walk away.**

Eighteen months ago Cameron left. Left Twin Rivers. Left his friends. Left her, Peyton Callahan.

And she moved on. The accident that took her brother's life ripped her world apart. The one person who could understand wasn't there, and Peyton hated him for it.

When he shows up back in town, all she wants to do is prove how well she recovered without him, how little she thinks about the past.

**But her past... well, he still thinks about her.**

# Chapter One

## PEYTON

---

~ *Pey,*

*I'm not coming back. You need to forget about me.*

*Cam* ~

---

*Cameron is missing.*

Eighteen months ago, those three little words changed Peyton Callahan's life forever. Everything that came after was like a punch in the gut, one right after another.

*Your brother is dead. Our rescue crew found Cooper's body in the wreckage at the bottom of Defiance Falls.*

They'd found her best friend, Cameron, the next morning. He went over the falls with Cooper, but he'd made it out of the car first. He washed up on the river bank miles away from the sight of the crash. He was unconscious, with a badly broken leg and a dangerous fever, but alive.

After Cooper's funeral, Julian, his twin, had left to go live with his aunt. Peyton knew it was hard for him walking around with Cooper's face, seeing the regret in everyone around him, and hearing the wrong twin had died. She knew he needed the escape, but that left Peyton alone to deal with their parents' grief along with her own.

But the final blow threw Peyton over the edge. After he was discharged from the hospital, Cameron—her lifelong best friend—left her too. His dad claimed they sent him to work with a world-class physical therapist to get him back in shape. She hadn't even had a chance to tell him goodbye.

Now, eighteen months later, Cooper was still dead and Julian was still gone while Cameron was off at some Olympic Training Center chasing his gold medal dreams.

"You've been polishing that same spot for the last ten minutes," Peyton's mother said as she stepped behind the diner counter, taking inventory of the coffee supplies. "Either wipe the whole counter or go clock out for dinner. And cancel your plans. I need you to work the late shift with me."

"Again?" she groaned. "I need to work on my STEM project tonight."

"On a Friday night?" Her mom's eyes filled with pity. "Don't you have anything better to do?"

Peyton scowled at her mother. Right she may be, but ouch. Once upon a time, Peyton had no shortage of friends and frequent weekend plans. Things changed after that night, and so had Peyton. Her STEM—Science, Technology, Engineering and Mathematics—project had saved her sanity over the last few months. It gave her something to focus on besides her grief.

"Go get dinner," her mother said in a softer tone. "We

have some healthy new salads and vegan meals on the menu. You've been doing so well lately. Don't let all the fried foods here tempt you. I'm proud of you." Her words were kind, but there was no emotion behind them. Ever since the death of her stepson—whom she'd loved like a son since he was six years old—Sofia Callahan went through the motions of being a mother. She was like a robot, and the only thing that seemed to matter to her anymore was her work at the diner she owned with her husband, Brian, Peyton's stepfather. Her parents threw themselves into working at the Main Street Diner. The Main was everyone's favorite restaurant in Twin Rivers, thanks to Sofia's blend of Spanish and American dishes along with her extensive dessert menu.

It made it difficult for Peyton's diet to be around such great food all the time, but she was doing so much better these days. She was making healthier choices and felt like the old Peyton was finally resurfacing again.

Peyton clocked out and put in her order for a roasted veggie sandwich with goat cheese on whole grain bread with a small side of vegan mac and cheese. It was a high carb day, so she got to pick all the healthy carbs. Tomorrow would be a low carb day of mostly veggies and lean proteins. Peyton had found carb cycling a diet plan she could live with and still achieve good results.

*And I'm under my calorie allotment for the day!* She might even have enough calories left over to squeeze in a dessert of frozen yogurt on the way home.

Peyton tapped her iPad screen and launched the app she was working on for the STEM competition she'd entered a few months ago. To enter the preliminary round, she'd had to develop a social networking app or website designed to promote positive online experiences among high school students. The project was right up Peyton's alley. She was good at coding and had an eye for web and app design. And she had a cause that drove her passion for the project.

Four months ago, she'd created the idea for No Body Shame, which she called No BS. The idea was for a social networking app, just for the students of her school. The app would provide a completely anonymous place where students could come to talk about body issues, labels and stereotypes, and how they affected people. Peyton hadn't expected much, but out of all the submissions in her school district, No BS was chosen, and Peyton had received a small stipend to create her app and submit it to the statewide competition over the summer break. She'd spent most of the summer building her app's infrastructure and had launched the beta app on the Twin Rivers High website more than a month ago.

To her complete surprise, her fellow students were actually using it. She was able to collect enough data and examples to submit for the state level competition and won first place! Now she was gearing up for the national STEM competition next month. She tried not to think about the grand prize scholarship to her college of choice. She didn't want to get her hopes up, but No BS was gaining in popularity, and Peyton spent all of her free time responding to comments and monitoring conversations. No BS had to maintain a positive user experience. That was the whole point. She would not tolerate cyberbullying of any kind, and she was working with her friend Katie and her mother on the security aspects of the app. She wanted to guarantee anonymity, but she still didn't have the budget for that. Katie's mom was helping her build a decent security system. She wasn't ready for nationals yet. But she was close. Peyton was so proud of her accomplishments, but more than anything, she was grateful for the distraction No BS gave her. When the memories got to be too much, she poured everything she had into the app. And for months now, No BS filled the empty void where her friends used to be.

---

*I love this app! It's such a relief to come here and see how many girls (and boys!) are dealing with the same issues I've dealt with for so long. I used to think I was alone. That there was no way anyone could understand what I went through last year. Some of the boys in my class started calling me "butterface." At first, I didn't know what it meant, but it didn't take long for the humiliation to sink in. Apparently, I have a great body ... ButHerFace... I just didn't realize I had an ugly face. I'm not a perfect beauty queen and I've never tried to be anything other than what I am. (I'm certainly not an ogre) The constant jerky remarks about putting a bag over my head had me begging my parents to send me to Defiance Academy next year. But after hanging out here, I've decided I will not let them shame me. I'm proud of who I am and I have a lovely face. Thank you No BS!*
—**@MyFaceIsMyFace**

---

*@MyFaceIsMyFace Don't you let those idiot boys run you away from your school. You hold your head high and show them how amazing you are inside and out.*
—**@ChocolateIsLife #EndBodyShamingNow**

---

*@MyFaceIsMyFace,@ChocolateIsLife is right #TheFuture-IsFemale*
—**@GirlsRock2019**

---

Peyton's heart nearly burst at the user's comment and positive replies. It still astounded her that so many people were using her app. No BS was exactly what so many young adults needed. She just prayed she could keep the cyberbullies away.

---

*—@MyFaceIsMyFace #GuysAreIdiots. Especially teenage boys who travel in packs. I guarantee if you showed an interest in any of them, they'd be thrilled. Keep your chin up and don't let anyone's words have that much power over you.#WeGotYou #NoBS*
—**@CupcakesAreMyNemesis, @NoBSmod**

---

"Ashley, you're so bad!" Peyton looked up at the familiar laugh. The hairs rose on the back of her neck at the sight of her former friend. "But you have the best stories." Addison Parker slid into the seat next to Peyton without acknowledging her presence. Addison was too busy with her cheerleader friends to notice.

"Peyton, honey, can you clock back in and wait on your friends?" her mom asked in a rush. "I have two waitresses late for their shifts, and we're filling up."

"Sure." Peyton slid off the bar stool where she'd sat, not

bothering to remind her mother these girls were not her friends. Addie used to be one of her closest friends, but not since that night. Gone were the days when Addison Parker fussed over Peyton's makeup and when Peyton's slow burn romance with Cameron was the topic of almost every after-school conversation. After Cooper's death, their friendship fell apart, and Addie moved on to new friends. Meaner friends.

"Hi, guys," Peyton said brightly, forcing a cheerful tone. "What can I get you?" She stood poised with her order pad on the counter, refusing to look at Addie. It hurt too much to see the cold insensitivity there.

"I'm starving," Ashley said. "I could eat a whole plate of chili cheese fries all by myself."

"Gross," Addison said. "Can you imagine the calories?"

Peyton coughed to cover her laughter. She'd seen Addie eat her weight in chili cheese fries more often than she could count.

"You're right. We should do salads," Ashley agreed. "It would be so nice not to care about our weight like you, Peyton. Just look at that hamburger and mac and cheese she was chowing down on before we got here. It looks so divine. But willpower, ladies. I'll have a half Cobb salad with ranch dressing on the side."

"Would you like steak, ham, or turkey?"

"Obviously, turkey," Ashley said as if that would make up for the mounds of cheese and bacon she'd neglected to substitute.

"I'll have the same," the other girls echoed.

"Anything else?" Peyton asked in a bored tone, not bothering to point out that her meal had a quarter of the calories of the diner salads they were about to inhale.

"Let's split some breadsticks. One for each of us," Veronica added. "I haven't had carbs in ages."

"Just this once," Ashley agreed like she was allowing it against her better judgment. "We've hit the gym pretty hard this week." She eyed Peyton's phone. "I suppose we could have been bingeing Netflix like some people, but we *are* in peak physical condition. A little bread won't kill us."

Peyton wanted to defend herself and point out she was the one eating the healthy food here and she was working on building something incredible—something they all used— not watching Netflix on her phone. But it wasn't worth it. They wouldn't believe her anyway. She turned toward the kitchen to put in their order when Ashley's next words hit her like a truck.

"We'll have to watch it over the next few weeks before school starts, ladies. Rumor has it Cameron Tucker is returning from the Olympic Village in Emerson. After more than a year training for the Olympic track team he'll be looking like a god and it's our job to help him integrate back into the social world of Twin Rivers High.

In a panic, Peyton gathered her dishes, tossing her half-eaten meal in the trash. Her hands trembled as she caught Addison's eyes for just a moment. For one second, she thought she saw sympathy there, and then it was gone.

Peyton raced into the bathroom at the back of the kitchen, her heart hammering in her chest. After eighteen months, Cameron was coming home. She looked at herself in the mirror, and disgust and self-loathing gazed back at her.

"I can't see him like this." She eyed her fuller figure. After Cooper's death and the destruction that came after, Peyton, always a curvy girl, had turned to food for comfort. In her grief, she hadn't cared. By the time she started noticing the world carrying on around her again, the damage was done. She'd gained more than fifty pounds, and none of her clothes fit her anymore. Not even her fat jeans. After months of diet and exercise, she'd lost some weight, but she still had a long way to go.

Peyton closed her eyes, refusing to look at herself any longer. She remembered how awful it felt the first time she had to buy a dress from the plus-sized department. She'd vowed she'd die before she'd ever shop on the fat side of the store. Now she had no other choice.

She couldn't bear the thought of seeing Cameron again. The last time they were together, their lifelong friendship was turning into much more. But there was no way Cameron Tucker—track god and Olympic hopeful—would ever look at her the same as he had that night after such a perfect first kiss. The girl he kissed that night didn't exist anymore.

Peyton jog-walked in the darkness around the school track. It was late, but she couldn't face going home. Not until she worked off the calories from a dinner of too many carbs. She pushed herself to go faster. Thoughts of seeing Cameron again drove her like she had a demon hot on her tail.

She'd thought she had come to terms with her lot as the fat girl. It had been that way her whole life, and for most of it, Peyton was strong enough to rise above the petty body shaming and find a level of confidence in herself that never

MICHELLE MACQUEEN & ANN MAREE CRAVEN

wavered. But after gaining so much weight since she'd last seen Cam, how was she ever going to face him?

Being the fat girl was nothing new. Peyton was in third grade when she first realized what made her different from everyone else. The thing that made her lesser somehow. She was only eight years old the first time the F word came to haunt her. Now, nearly a decade later, she could still remember the name of the classmate—a *friend*—who'd shattered her illusions about herself. *Allison.* It was ancient history, but her words cut deep into Peyton's eight-year-old soul. Peyton and Allison were in the girls' bathroom with a bunch of their classmates. Allison spoke to her from another stall.

"How much do you weigh, Peyton?"

"Um, I don't know," Peyton said.

"You know you're fat, right? Like twice the size of anyone else in our grade?"

Young Peyton didn't have a response to such harsh words. Of course, she knew she was bigger than most of her friends; she wasn't blind. But she hadn't realized her size gave others a license to ridicule her. Apparently, that made it okay … because Peyton was fat.

Then in sixth grade, PE class with Coach Anderson was a living nightmare. Every day, filled with anxiety, Peyton headed to the gym with her classmates for her ritual hazing … from the teacher who had the best opportunity of anyone to help her overcome her weight problem before it became a lifelong struggle.

Twelve years old and Peyton had to answer to the name "Big Mac" during roll call. She wasn't the only one with weight issues. Peyton remembered a "Pat-the-fat" and an "Amanda-big-boned" in her class that year too—all names brought to life by the illustrious Coach Anderson. There were others who didn't perform well athletically, but they got to respond to their actual names in class. But it was okay ... because Peyton was fat.

Coach Anderson started every class with running laps. If you couldn't make it three laps around the gym without stopping or walking, you got more laps. Some days, Peyton was forced to run-walk laps the entire period rather than play kickball or field hockey with her classmates. And then she went back to class sweaty and ashamed for being ostracized from her friends. But it was okay for a grown-ass man to shame a sixth grader because Peyton was fat and needed to learn that was not acceptable.

Peyton hated PE with every fiber of her being. And now, here she was running laps in the middle of the night like her life depended on it.

"I have four weeks left before school starts," she reminded herself, taking the last turn in the track as she slowed to a stop. One more month to lose some of the weight she'd put on in Cameron's absence. "I can drop twenty pounds in that time if I really push it." Her calves burned, and she felt a little dizzy, but she had one more lap in her tonight. Peyton refused to be the fat girl anymore.

# Chapter Two

## CAMERON

---

*~ Cam*
*I want you to know you can do anything.*
*Peyton ~*

---

The stars used to hold every possibility. Cameron Tucker would lie in bed at night watching the cheap glowing stickers on his ceiling. They were childish, but he'd never been able to bring himself to take them down.

*I want you to know you can do anything.*

Those had been the words of his best friend, Peyton, when she was ten years old. She'd always been there when he doubted himself.

But he'd left those stars behind, and they now felt farther away than ever. He couldn't do anything. Not anymore.

With a sigh, he rolled onto his side. Had his bed always

been this uncomfortable? Was his room always depressing?

Eighteen months ago, he'd left home and wasn't sure he'd return. He never even had the chance to say goodbye to the people who were only sort of his friends. The only guy he'd been close with was dead. And he hadn't called the girl his absence would hurt the most.

Eighteen months. Enough time for the Cameron Tucker who'd lived in their small town to disappear. He closed his eyes, wanting the silence only sleep could bring. It was no use. The memories he'd fought so hard to forget were a constant presence now that he'd returned.

Light crept around the edges of his curtains, but he didn't know what time it was. School didn't start for a few weeks yet, and he was perfectly content staying in his bed until then.

A knock on his door ruined that possibility. Before he could answer, his mother poked her head in. The tentative smile on her face was just another reminder of how much things had changed. His parents hadn't known what to say to him since he'd arrived home the day before.

"Hi, sweetie." Her sad eyes swept the bare walls of his room. The first thing he'd done when he got home was remove the posters belonging to the kid who'd lost everything in a single night. Her smile tightened. "I made you a smoothie. You didn't eat dinner last night, so I expect you downstairs in five minutes."

She shut the door without waiting for a response. Five minutes? Was she kidding? Cam was no longer in the "roll out of bed and throw on some pants" stage of his life. It took him much longer than that to pull himself together enough to face the world. But she didn't know. How could she? His parents had only visited him once during his time away.

Twenty minutes later, he entered the kitchen. His father sat at the table with a newspaper hiding his face. He didn't lower it or acknowledge Cam. Unlike Cam's mother, his father wasn't an actor. He couldn't pretend things were as they'd always been.

And Cam was grateful for that small mercy. He didn't know how to speak to his father anymore either. For most of his life, their relationship was based on running. They were coach and athlete, both with a dream of making it to the Olympics.

When the only dream you had died, part of you went with it.

Cam's mother handed him one of her healthy smoothies. He definitely hadn't missed this. He'd spent so many years choking them down he just couldn't do it anymore. This time, as he took a sip, he cringed at the chalky taste of too much protein powder. It was worse than he remembered.

He attempted a smile. "Thanks, Mom." He grabbed his keys off the hook on the wall.

"Where are you going?" She wiped her hands on her apron. "I thought we could do some school shopping today."

Nope. He couldn't do it. She tried so hard to treat him like he was still her normal son, and it made him feel like he was anything but.

He only shook his head and left his parents behind. Outside, he dumped his smoothie into a bush and threw the empty cup into the back of his car before climbing in.

He hadn't planned where he was going, but there was a route he knew better than any other.

Sun beat down on him through his windshield. It must have been ninety degrees. He wiped sweaty palms on his black sweatpants and gripped the steering wheel.

Twin Rivers never changed. The whole town was stuck in some nightmare time warp. Two streets over from Cam's house was Main Street where residents and tourists walked from crappy knickknack store to crappy antique store. The Anderson family had owned the hardware shop for three generations.

Even the Main Street Diner... He averted his eyes as he passed the familiar building. Grandpa Callahan opened it four decades ago and passed it to his grandson when he died. Cam knew every inch of that restaurant.

He wondered if Peyton Callahan was in there serving the early customers, her smile brightening their mornings. Cam had once told her she smiled too much. He hadn't meant it. He'd just been teasing. She'd laughed and asked him why she shouldn't smile. He hadn't had an answer other than he'd secretly wanted her to reserve her goodness only for him. He'd been selfish that way. But he'd never told her how he felt, not until it was too late.

He slowed and finally let his eyes rest on the diner. Through the window, he saw Mrs. Callahan standing at the counter probably poring over receipts.

Being a part of their family was another thing he'd lost. Peyton would never forgive him for the way he'd left when she'd needed him the most. Even if she did, she deserved more than a best friend who was broken beyond repair. His breath clogged in his throat as Mrs. Callahan lifted her head and peered out the window as if she could sense him. Those eyes... That woman... She'd always had kind words and a warm home for him. She hadn't deserved to lose her son.

He tore his gaze away and continued down the road, turning out of the downtown area—if you could call it that. The road wound down toward the tumultuous convergence of the two rivers before inching up toward Defiance Falls. Cam suddenly couldn't breathe.

Drowning. He was drowning. He sucked in a breath as if it would expel the imagined water from his lungs and pressed the gas pedal to the floor. The car lurched forward, taking the narrow road at a speed he knew was too fast. But he had to get past it. He had to get away from the dark water and frothing falls. The droning of his car overcame the crash of water below.

After a few minutes, he slammed on the brakes, coming to a screeching halt.

He rested his forehead on the steering wheel, hearing their voices in his mind. *We have to get out of here. Cam, get Avery to the shore. I'm not leaving without my brother.*

But he had. Cooper Callahan had still been in the car when it went over the falls while Julian Callahan made it out. Cam tried to help Cooper. After getting Avery to shore, he'd jumped back into the water, but the current was too strong, and he hadn't made it back to the car before it tumbled over the edge.

He slammed his head against the hard leather of his steering wheel, and his horn blared. Calming his breathing, he reached behind his seat for the box that was always there. The last time he'd been with Peyton, she'd given him a small wooden box containing notes she'd written in her girlish handwriting. She'd said they were encouragement for when he needed it. That was before the accident that changed their lives. He'd left the gift behind, but Peyton brought it to the hospital. Cam's dad refused her entry but accepted the present.

Cam hadn't been able to make himself look at a single note, but he'd kept the box with him always. First, in his many hospital rooms and rehab facilities. Eventually, when he could drive again, it lived on the back seat, almost as if she too was there.

He ran his fingers over the carved wood, letting it soothe his nerves as he always did. *Breathe, son. Breathe.* The paramedic's words that night never left him, and he did as he was told. *Keep breathing. Don't let yourself disappear. It will be okay.*

He set the box on the seat beside him and pulled his BMW back onto the road. The car had been a present from his parents. They thought it would make him feel better. Normal people sent flowers or maybe a balloon.

What they didn't understand was nothing could replace what he'd lost. Nothing could fix him.

The school came into view. In a few short weeks, he'd be there for his senior year. If it was up to him, he'd have continued his online schooling. But nothing was up to him.

He parked in the small lot next to the football stadium. A track wrapped around the field, and the familiar scene sent more pain through him than he thought he could feel anymore. But he couldn't walk away.

A few people lingered nearby, and some ran morning laps. Cam didn't know if he was just paranoid or if their eyes really followed him. With any luck, they would barely notice his return. But he wasn't the lucky sort, and the accident had changed their small town.

On the field, the football team ran suicides. He hated football, yet he envied them. The black Tartan turf of the track held a familiar peace under Cam's feet. He used to think it was where he was meant to be.

Now, it represented a past he wanted to forget. Cam walked around the track to the bleachers and climbed up a few rows before sitting down. He recognized a few kids from the track team but didn't approach them. He wasn't one of them anymore.

In truth, without running, he didn't know where he fit anymore.

He bowed his head and ran a hand through his shaggy brown hair. At the far end of the bleachers, a girl ran the steps. Cam lifted his eyes to watch her, a familiar yearning in his gut.

Peyton.

He knew he'd eventually see her but wasn't prepared for it to happen so soon. The last time he'd seen her had been the best night of his life...until it turned into the worst. And now, he couldn't separate the memory of finally admitting the feelings he'd had for years and the accident.

A big part of him had been relieved he was in the car with her brothers that night instead of her. But it was hard to feel that relief when he had to live with the consequences.

He closed his eyes, picturing the rickety tree house behind Addison Parker's house. It had just been the two of them. He'd had so much to apologize for that night. Avery and his football buddies had been making fun of Peyton's weight, and like an idiot, he didn't defend her.

He still hated himself for that.

*"Peyton." He wiped a tear from her face with his thumb. "You know I could never think..."*

*He couldn't actually say it, and he knew he'd been wrong to avoid it the moment he stopped speaking. Peyton shrank in to herself.*

*"Believe me, I know what people think of me." Her voice was quiet, but it wrapped around him like a cloak of sadness. "I've lived with it most of my life. I just thought..." She shook her head.*

*He leaned in. "What did you think?"*

*When she lifted her eyes, they shone with unshed tears. Her emotion slammed into him, stealing his breath away. Peyton had always kept her feelings carefully guarded. It wasn't the first time people had made fun of her. Their school was cruel. But she'd always kept a mask of uncaring coolness firmly in place. Now it had crumbled into dust, revealing the girl he'd only seen a few times throughout their childhood. Vulnerable. Fragile. And just as beautiful as the strong girl he'd always known.*

*Her eyes pleaded with him to take back his question. She couldn't lie to him, and something told him she didn't want to give him an answer.*

*He needed to know.*

*His eyes scanned her face as it reflected the shadows of the night. Silver moonlight bounced off the curves of her cheeks and the bridge of her nose. Her pale, frozen lips parted to release a puff of air.*

*"What did you think, Peyton?" He wasn't letting her avoid the question. Not this time.*

*Her brows pulled together as silence stretched between them. After a few tense moments, Peyton shocked Cam by leaning forward and pressing her lips to his.*

*He didn't respond at first as his mind worked faster than his body.*

*Peyton pulled away, rejection in her eyes.*

*Cam wanted to erase every bit of hurt he saw there, so he did the only thing he could. He pulled her back to him, melting her icy lips with his kiss.*

*A sigh escaped her.*

*Cam rose up on his knees to change the angle and deepen the kiss. His hands wound through her hair, tilting her head up as he took control.*

*Something clicked into place inside him, a rightness. His feelings for Peyton had been so confusing for months, and now, he knew why. She hadn't simply been his best friend, not in a long time. She'd been Peyton, the girl who owned a piece of him, who'd always cared for him.*

*"Cam," she whispered against his lips. "Is this real?" Her hands skimmed the width of his chest as if exploring him for the first time. Maybe it was the first time. They'd slept in the same bed for years and curled up against each other for movies.*

*But now they were strangers, getting to know new sides of each other.*

*"Yeah, Peyton." He leaned back, running his fingers down her face until they rested on her swollen lips. "This is real."*

*"You're still my best friend. You know that, right? This doesn't have to change anything."*

*He rested his forehead against hers. "This changes everything." His eyes slid shut. "Sorry it took me so long."*

*She laughed, and he snapped his eyes open, enjoying the sound. "I'm glad you find me amusing."*

*"Cam." She shook her head. "You're the most oblivious guy in the entire world. You don't know how wonderful you are. How many girls you leave brokenhearted by refusing to date. It's one of the things I like about you."*

*"Do you want to know what I like about you?"*

*She grinned. "Yes."*

*Honesty. He could be honest. Just this once. He'd never been good at sharing his feelings. Most people at school thought he was a robot, only caring about his next running time. They were wrong. He cared...so much. He just didn't know how to express it. No one had ever taught him. His parents gave him their single-minded drive, their ambition, but little else.*

*"You're kind," he began, a slow smile spreading across his face. "The kindest person I know. You can make me feel like the world isn't such a bad place, like I'll be okay if I don't achieve everything I've been working toward. When I'm with you, I see different things. My future isn't only clouded by Olympic rings. I don't know what's going to happen or if I'm going to make it, and that terrifies me sometimes. But every time you tell me it'll be okay, I believe it."*

*He cupped her cheek. "You make me fearless, Pey."*

Fearless. He shook his head. All he'd known since that night was fear. He should have spent the following months dreaming of Peyton and spending his days lost in her. Instead, his sleeping hours held nightmares of raging water and dying friends while his days held hard reminders that everything he'd felt before was now tainted with pain.

A loud thud ripped him from his dark thoughts, and he jumped to his feet as Peyton slammed face-first into the bleacher steps.

"I'm okay," she groaned, rolling onto her back.

At one time, he would have laughed at her clumsiness. Peyton had never been exactly graceful. But as he rushed to help her up and she lifted her eyes to meet his, he couldn't breathe.

Because Peyton Callahan was angry. And she hadn't changed at all.

# Chapter Three

## PEYTON

~ *Peyton,*

    *We aren't friends. Move on.*

    *Cam ~*

Peyton stared up into a pair of blue eyes she knew better than her own. The warmth of his hand wrapping around hers sent her heart hammering in her chest as Cameron Tucker helped her back on her feet. Her face flushed hot with embarrassment, both for her clumsy face-plant and for running into *him* at the worst possible moment.

I was supposed to have two more weeks! *She wasn't ready to see him again. Not like this. Hot and sweaty, wearing her crappy yoga pants and with unwashed hair—it wasn't fair. Not when he looked better than ever, and she'd only lost six pounds since she found out he was coming home.*

He was different. Older now. Taller, if that was even possible. His sandy-brown hair fell across the more mature plains of his face, and a light blond stubble covered his jawline. But those eyes. The way they looked right through her walls to see everything she was now. She drifted toward him, like her body refused to listen to her mind. She ached to be near him again. To feel his arms around her.

*How is it remotely fair he's even hotter now?* She wanted to stamp her foot, but Peyton just stood there on the bleachers, staring into his eyes as a wave of white-hot rage swept over her, washing away all the feelings she used to have for him.

She suddenly wanted to shove him and scream at him for abandoning her at the worst moment of her life. The old Peyton would have, but this Peyton wanted the earth to open up and swallow her so she wouldn't have to experience all the feelings seeing him again brought back.

"How could you leave me like that?" The words vomited out of her mouth before she thought about what she was saying. Embarrassment engulfed her once more as she turned to flee. He'd moved on over the last year. She couldn't let him see she was still stuck in her grief. Still stuck on him and that night. That kiss that no longer meant anything.

"Peyton, wait!" he called behind her, but she tucked her earbuds back into her ears and ran for her car. She wasn't ready to face him. Too much had changed.

Peyton's empty stomach gurgled as she filled it with ice water. She eyed the contents of the refrigerator, looking for anything that had fewer than a hundred calories.

"I'm so sick of thinking about calories." She sighed as she grabbed a triple protein Greek yogurt that tasted like butt. It would tide her over to her next bland meal.

"Peyton? That you?"

The yogurt slipped out of her hand at the sound of Cooper's voice. The sight of her dead brother's smiling face sent a flood of tears to her eyes. Constant hunger made her vision a little blurry, but seeing ghosts was never a good thing. Then she noticed his blue eye, and a light switched on inside her. "Julian?" she screeched as she ran across the kitchen to hug her very much alive brother. Cooper's twin was his identical match in every way except one. Julian had heterochromia which affected the color of his eyes. He had one brown eye and one blue. Cooper's eyes were both brown. It was the only way to tell the twins apart when they were trying to fool you.

She clung to him like a lifeline. "I've missed you so much!" Her tears leaked onto his shirt as he wrapped his arms around her.

"Me too, little sis," he whispered, dropping a kiss on top of her head.

"Are you home, home?" She leaned back to get a good look at him. He looked good. She couldn't deny the time away was probably what he'd needed. *But what about what I needed?* The selfish thought took root in her mind, freeing the anger she'd felt toward Julian for more than a year. Yes, Cooper was his twin, but they'd both lost a brother that night. It didn't matter to her they weren't her brothers by blood. In her heart, they were her family. Losing Cooper had crushed her as much as it had Julian.

"Looks that way." He sighed.

"What about college?" She frowned. Julian wasn't the best

student, but he'd planned to do a year at the local community college before trying to transfer to a state university.

"Gotta finish high school first."

"What?"

"I didn't do so well last year, so it looks like we'll be seniors together this year."

"Oh, Julian, I'm sorry," she said. "You should have told me you were struggling with school. I could have helped."

"You kind of have to go to school to find out what the assignments are." He shrugged, taking a seat at the kitchen counter. "It's so good to see you, Peyton." He pulled her into the seat beside him. "I have a surprise." He pulled a white bakery box from under the counter.

"Oh no," Peyton said. "Whatever's in that box is not my friend."

"What?" Julian gave her a look. "I've never known Peyton Callahan to say no to Mom's strawberry cheesecake cupcakes." He pulled the adorable pink cupcakes out of the box emblazoned with The Main Street Diner logo. They were ooey-gooey and pink with flecks of real strawberries in the mile-high icing.

"Do you know how long I've been dreaming about these?" He was almost drooling, so he didn't see the look of terror on Peyton's face.

"I take it Mom made them for your homecoming?" she asked nervously.

"I had to talk her into it. She doesn't like making them."

"Because they're so fattening."

"Because they're so delicious." Julian dove into his cupcake, the pink icing smearing his upper lip like a milk mustache. "Come on. I've been waiting for you to get home so we can share the joy."

"I'm not eating that," Peyton insisted, but she couldn't take her eyes off the tantalizing cake. It was like waving heroin in front of an addict, but Julian had no idea this particular cupcake was her drug of choice.

"You have to, sis." He shoved a cupcake under her nose, smearing the icing on her lips.

"You're such an jerk." She smiled and took a small bite. *Just half won't kill me.*

"Yeah, I am. Welcome home, right?" He grinned at her, tapping his second cupcake to hers like a toast.

"Why didn't anyone tell me you were coming home?" she asked, trying to keep her focus on him and not the oh-so-stupid-good cake that just tanked her calories for the whole day. Because Peyton Callahan couldn't just eat half. She sighed, wishing for the days when moderation in everything was her motto. She'd been happy then. Even if she wasn't a size two.

"I wasn't sure I was coming, to be honest." He leaned back against the chair. "Part of me just wanted to get my GED and move on. Get a job and forget about…everything."

"I know that feeling," Peyton agreed.

"You weren't there, kid," he said, shaking his head.

"Bull, Julian," she snapped. "I might not have been in the accident with you, but I lost everything that night. Even you." She picked at the empty cupcake wrapper. *And it's all my fault. I'm the one who sent them away that night.* She wouldn't blame Julian if he never forgave her.

"I'm sorry I left you like that. I just couldn't deal with being in this town wearing his face, knowing everyone— even our own parents—wished it had gone the other way."

"That's not true. I know you were hurting, but so was I. I needed you, and you just abandoned me." She reached for a second cupcake without thinking. "You lost a brother that night, but I lost *both* of my brothers, my parents…and every friend I ever had. What happened in that car, Julian?" She turned pleading eyes on him.

"Nothing." Julian shoved his chair back. "Absolutely nothing." He stalked off toward his bedroom, slamming the door behind him.

# Chapter Four

## CAMERON

~ Cam,

    *You know the best thing about having Cameron Tucker as a best friend?*

    *You always know exactly what I need.*

    *Peyton ~*

The red-brick building shone in the blazing sun as students ran across the grassy lawn. People sat around picnic tables, buzzing with excitement as friends reunited after a long summer apart.

Cam had been gone for more than a summer, yet the idea of being around the kids he'd gone to school with since he was six years old held no appeal. Twin Rivers was a town where every student knew each other. Their parents knew each other. Even their grandparents in many cases.

He caught the eye of a group of girls he'd always had to avoid before. They constantly wanted something from him, the Olympic hopeful.

This time, they didn't approach, but their eyes followed him across the grassy expanse. He hiked his backpack farther onto his shoulder and stopped when he reached the stone pathway.

Something hard rammed into his shoulder, sending him sprawling forward. He caught himself before eating pavement and cursed. He dropped his backpack and made sure his pant leg didn't ride up as the crowd of jersey-clad footballers laughed and continued walking. Just what he needed —for them to see how damaged he'd returned.

He picked up his bag and slung it over his shoulder as his eyes found the one jock who wasn't laughing. Avery St. Germaine had always walked the line between jerk and friend. One of those, it seemed, had won out over the other.

Avery shook ash-brown hair out of his eyes and looked away, his lips pressed into a thin line.

Cam shouldn't have expected any different. Being in an accident together wasn't exactly a bonding experience. If anything, it did more to tear them apart.

He clenched his jaw and started forward, yet again, only to stop as he took in the sight at the table nearest the door. He stumbled back, shaking his head. After squeezing his eyes shut, he opened them again, unable to look away from Julian Callahan.

Cam had heard from the letters their friend Nari insisted on sending him that Julian had disappeared from Twin Rivers just as he had. That wasn't what had Cam's chest constricting.

Julian and Cooper were identical twins, only set apart by

their eyes and their personalities. Every other little detail had been the same.

Tears gathered in Cam's eyes, but he refused to let them fall. He'd cried once right after the accident and then never again.

*"Cam, get Avery out of here. Get to shore." Julian wedged his feet against the door for leverage as he pulled at the strap across his twin's chest.*

*"We're getting too close to the falls." Cam held Avery's unconscious form above the rising water in the back seat of the car. Panic raced through him, but he couldn't just leave. "You need my help."*

*The roar of the falls drowned out Julian's next words, but he gripped the crowbar he'd used to get into the car and raised it above his head in clear threat.*

Julian hadn't been in the car with them, but he'd followed behind and hadn't hesitated in jumping into the river to help them. He hadn't saved his brother, but Cam knew the only reason he and Avery were walking around school today was because Julian threatened to hit Cam with a crowbar if he didn't leave the car.

And yet, he couldn't stop imagining it was Cooper sitting at that table, head bent over a book. Inky hair fell into Julian's eyes, and he brushed it away without ceasing his reading.

No one approached him, and he didn't lift his head.

Cam's breath came out in short bursts as if he'd run the entire way to school. His heart hammered against his chest, and sweat dotted his brow. *Cooper was gone. Cooper was gone.* He had to repeat it to himself over and over to stop the panic from consuming him. The crash of water rang in his ears.

He shook his head. "I can't do this."

"Yes, you can." He hadn't sensed her presence until the voice of Nari Won Song overcame everything else.

He turned to find the tiny girl standing behind him. She pushed thick-framed glasses up her narrow nose and stared at him with those dark all-knowing eyes of hers. His heart rate slowed.

Nari had been Peyton's best friend and, by extension, his.

"Hey, Cam." She smiled and pushed her straight black hair behind one ear. Her other arm clutched her books.

He opened his mouth to speak but couldn't find the words. Nari had been the only one of their group who knew where he was the past eighteen months. She'd badgered his mother to get his address. Her letters came every month like clockwork. A normal person would have written emails, but she wasn't normal. His therapist found out about the letters and made him read them in front of her. She'd thought reconnecting with his old life would help with his recovery.

"I got your letters." It was all he could think of to say.

Nari smiled. Not wide like Peyton once did. Her smiles were shy, small.

"I'm sorry I didn't respond." He fixed his eyes on the ground.

She shrugged. "I didn't expect you to, Cam. I just didn't want us to lose you too. We all used to be so close, but now, it's like we don't know each other at all.

After the..." She paused. "After that night, you and Julian both just disappeared. Peyton may as well have for how much she retreated into herself. Avery acts as if he never knew us. Addison has become everything she claimed she never would. And Cooper..." She didn't finish that sentence.

Cam scrubbed a hand over his face. "You can't fix us, Nari."

"Why not?" She stuck her lip out. "I want to try. It's been over a year, and this is our last year all together here in Twin Rivers."

Cam's eyes tracked a girl as she ran across the lawn, trying to avoid being late. She stopped when she caught sight of them, her feet frozen in place. Nari's gaze followed his, and she sighed. "Have you talked to her?"

Cam didn't take his eyes from Peyton. "You want to know why you can't fix us, Nari?" He turned away. "Because there's nothing left to fix. Every bond we all had with each other now lays at the bottom of the river."

He walked back the way he'd come, and Nari didn't follow him. He thought he'd be able to face school, but he'd been wrong. It would still be there tomorrow.

His bright red car stood out in the parking lot like a beacon, calling him to better places. He threw his bag in the back seat and climbed in.

This time, when he reached the river, he didn't speed past it. Instead, he pulled off the road, slowed to a stop, and got out, slamming his door behind him. The sounds of the road faded as he walked toward the edge of the rushing water. The falls weren't far.

A breeze whipped through the clearing, bending the thin reeds at the edge of the water. The panic Cam expected to feel never came. He lowered himself to the grassy bank, his eyes transfixed by the swift current.

A mile upriver, the second river crossed this one in a wide and rocky convergence. Cam had always preferred the narrower parts where large trees lined the banks, hanging their branches over the water. As kids, they'd spent their summers boating and swimming in the river. Most people in town had. One of Nari's letters told him the town forbade swimming in the current the summer after the accident.

Cooper Callahan had been the town golden boy, Twin Rivers' chance at glory as he would have gone on to play college football for Ohio State. He'd been a junior when he died and already recruited.

"Coop." Cam rested his forearms on his knees and leaned forward. "I miss you, man. Nothing is the same without you here."

He closed his eyes, imagining Cooper giving Peyton and Julian endless trouble. None of them had any illusions what kind of man Cooper had been, but Cam only wanted to remember the good. The way he could amp up any party. The way he and Julian protected Peyton.

For a long time after the accident, Cam had tried to figure out exactly what happened that night. Why they'd been in that car with a drunk Cooper driving. Cooper had been kicked out of the party, but why?

He wanted to blame Peyton for telling Coop to leave, but she hadn't started the fight. Yet, blaming a dead guy seemed pointless despite Cam's need to pin his hurt on someone.

Rationally, he knew Cooper shouldn't have driven. Avery had been in no shape to argue, but Cam had. Was it his fault for not insisting he drive? Even though he hadn't realized Coop was drunk until it was too late.

So many questions swirled in his mind. He'd probably never know all the events leading up to the accident. Maybe he didn't want to. He was pretty sure Cooper had done something bad before getting into the car, and he didn't want to remember him like that.

"I need your help, Coop." Cam lifted his eyes to the clear sky above. "I don't want to be this angry forever."

He absently rubbed his hand down his pant leg until it hit metal. "None of them know, buddy." He lifted his pant leg to reveal the workings of the prosthetic leg they told him would one day feel like a part of him. News flash: It didn't. He still had a foreign object attached to his body. Other than the doctors, only his parents knew. Not the reporters who'd followed his Olympic training so closely. Not the people he'd once called friends. They didn't know why he left after the accident and if he had any say, they never would.

But he needed to talk to someone, and at least Cooper didn't interrupt. "I woke up in the hospital three days after the accident, and part of my leg was gone. They'd amputated below the knee. I don't remember much from my time in the water, but they say I had a deep laceration when they found me the day after going over the falls. Infection had spread through the tissue of my calf. The amputation was lifesaving, they claimed." His back shook. "You're dead, Coop, and yet when I woke, I felt like I'd lost my life as well. How horrible am I?" He shook his head. "I'd appreciate if you didn't tell anyone." He wiped his face, and a small smile appeared almost as if he'd forgotten he had no reason to smile.

Cooper couldn't actually hear him, but it eased some of the burden to let someone else hold his secrets. He got to his feet, letting his pant leg drift down to cover his false leg.

When he got back into his car, the air didn't feel as thick as it had before. He leaned his head back and closed his eyes. He'd faced the river, faced Cooper, and he'd survived it.

Tomorrow, he resolved, he'd face school and all the people he'd left behind.

# Chapter Five

## PEYTON

~ *Peyton,*

*I think about you, a lot. And I don't want to. I don't want to miss you. It hurts too much. We can never go back.*

*Cam* ~

Peyton rushed to get to her locker before first period. The first week of her senior year wasn't going so well. She'd avoided both Cameron and Julian whenever possible, but her energy was dragging from her twice daily workouts, too little food, and not nearly enough sleep. Peyton was doing all the unhealthy things she swore she'd never do to lose weight. And it wasn't even working.

*I just need to lose thirty more pounds, and I'll be back to my regular pudgy self, and then I can work on maintaining.* She slammed her locker door, taking a bite of her tasteless, organic, ninety-calorie protein bar and turned around, practically running right into Addison and her mini-mes.

"Jeez, Peyton," Addison said. "Can't you stop eating for once in your life?"

Peyton scrambled to heft her backpack on her shoulder so she could remove the foil-wrapped breakfast bar hanging from her mouth.

"Honestly, you should be more careful about what you eat," Ashley said, giving Peyton a disgusted look.

"It's only a—" But the girls wouldn't let her finish.

"Seriously, it's for your own good," Veronica said with a snicker as they drifted off to their first period classes.

Peyton struggled to swallow the bland offensive bite.

"Silly me," she muttered. "I forgot I'm not allowed to eat in public." She wiped her mouth, staring at the perfect slim figures of Twin Rivers High's resident mean girls. It didn't matter she was starving. It didn't matter she was eating something healthy on the go. Fat people didn't get to eat like other people. In peace and without shame.

"How much weight have you lost, Peyton?"

Peyton winced at the sound of a kind voice. Katie Whitmore. Undoubtedly, the quietest girl in their school—but she still somehow managed to also be one of the nicest people Peyton had ever met.

"Twenty-eight pounds," Peyton said. "And apparently not enough."

"You look great," Katie said. "Keep up the good work, and don't let the mean girls tear you down. You're almost there." She beamed a big smile at Peyton before she left for her first class.

"Thanks." *I think.* Almost there? What did that even mean? Almost small enough to be considered a real person again? Where was that invisible line between normal and unacceptably fat? In Peyton's grief, she'd missed the day she'd crossed that line.

It was like she'd fallen into the twilight zone. Somehow her weight gain had pushed her into an alternate world where it was suddenly okay to insult a person to their face— for their own good. A world where even the nicest people, with the best intentions, gave backhanded compliments.

With a sigh, Peyton tossed the other half of her breakfast into the trash, wishing she lived in a simple world where it was okay to just be herself, no matter her size.

"You're late," Ms. Miller snapped when Peyton shuffled into her second period English lit class a moment after the bell. "Take a seat."

"Sorry." This was the worst part of her school day. As luck would have it, she was stuck sitting between the two people she wanted to avoid like the plague. Neither Cameron nor Julian met her gaze as she slid into her seat between them. They each worked hard not to speak to one another throughout the period, but it ruined her favorite subject.

Halfway through the class, Peyton's stomach growled, and she had trouble focusing on Ms. Miller's lecture, thinking about the banana and almonds she had stashed in her locker for her afternoon snack.

Finally, she raised her hand. "May I have the hall pass?"

With a nod from Ms. Miller, Peyton darted into the hall. She grabbed her snack from her locker and ducked into the bathroom.

She was going to regret this later when she was starving again, but she had to put something in her stomach, or she wasn't going to make it to her bland lunch of dry tuna and a small salad with a tiny portion of avocado and no dressing.

Peyton propped her feet up on the bathroom stall door and let out a sigh. Munching on her banana and almonds in peace. *Score! There's no fat shaming when you eat on the toilet.* She thought about eating lunch in there later, just for the peace and quiet, when she heard the bathroom door open. She saw Addie through the crack in the stall and stilled her movement. She wasn't in the mood for another humiliating slap in the face from her former friend.

Retching noises surprised her as Addie coughed and gagged in the next stall until she finally threw up.

*Oh, Addie, what are you doing to yourself?* Addison had always demanded perfection in her life. She was the ideal beauty in every possible way, but it never seemed good enough for Addison. *Was this how she attained that level of perfection?* Peyton stared at her banana, thinking for a moment that maybe she was doing it wrong.

*Seriously, Peyton?* She chastised herself for even thinking about it. No amount of skinny was worth that price.

Just when Addie came up for air after purging the contents of her stomach, Peyton's bag of almonds slipped off her lap and onto the floor. *No!*

"Who's there?" Addison demanded, charging out of her stall.

"Sorry." Peyton sighed as she stepped out.

Addison rushed to the sink to wash her hands and wipe her mouth. Peyton eyed the telltale teeth marks along Addison's knuckles.

"Addie," Peyton whispered, taking a cautious step forward.

"What? I don't feel good." She shrugged, refusing to meet Peyton's gaze.

"Seriously, Addie? Why are you doing this to yourself? It's not worth it."

"I don't know what you're talking about." She focused on reapplying her lip gloss and then caught sight of the bag of almonds in Peyton's hand.

"Oh my gosh, really? You skipped out of class to eat in the bathroom?" She laughed, grabbing her purse off the bathroom counter. "You're pathetic, Peyton." She shoved past her, leaving Peyton alone wondering if maybe she was right.

After another silent lunch sitting with Katie Whitmore, Peyton was exhausted. The only person who seemed to be having a harder time of it was Julian. He sat alone in the cafeteria while his fellow seniors pelted him with paper, bits of food, and hateful comments. But Julian maintained an uncaring aura, reading his book with his feet up on the seat beside him like he didn't have a care in the world. They couldn't touch him.

If only she had it that easy.

As Peyton left to dump her trash, wishing for a cup of coffee to get her through the rest of the day, she heard Ashley's hateful voice.

"Why did he come back? I can't believe he's even showing his face here. We are all still mourning Cooper's death, and he's just an unwelcome reminder of what we've lost."

"Yeah," Addison absently agreed. "What a loss."

Peyton's blood boiled. She was so angry with Julian for leaving and for refusing to tell her anything about that night. But he was still her brother, and she still wanted to come to his defense and put Ashley in her place. How dare she try to own even a portion of the loss Peyton's whole family suffered with Cooper's death?

But Peyton wasn't strong enough for that kind of confrontation, so she put her head down and rushed for the cafeteria exit just as the bell rang. Her hands clenched into fists at her sides, she charged through the swinging doors and barreled right into Cameron.

He grabbed her arms, steadying her on her feet. "You okay?" he asked.

For a moment, the last eighteen months vanished, and Cameron's touch made her shiver in anticipation of his kiss. And then something broke inside her, freeing the rage she'd fought to suppress only moments before. "No! I'm not okay." She shoved him back a step. "Not that you even care!" she shouted as students poured into the halls. She shoved him again. It felt good. "How could you do it, Cameron? Huh?" It felt good to scream. She stepped toward him, but he clutched her arms.

"Peyton. No," he said. "Not here."

"Really? Not here?" She shouted louder this time. "What? You don't want everyone to know how you kissed me that night? How you told me you loved me, and then you just left? For eighteen months?" She pulled away from his grip, her eyes filling with tears. "You were supposed to be my best friend, Cameron Tucker." Her voice trembled as the hallway grew quiet and everyone stared. "My brother died! Julian left, and my entire world fell apart." She took a step back. "And you want to know the worst part?" She shook her head in disgust. "I learned my best friend—the boy I'd loved my whole life—was nothing but a coward." She stumbled back, unable to bear the hurt look on his face. Peyton whirled around and walked away, careless of the stares and murmurs following her. She'd had enough for one day.

# Chapter Six

## CAMERON

---

~ *Cam,*
   *Please don't hate me.*
   *Peyton* ~

---

*Nothing but a coward.*

Peyton didn't know the truth in her words. Cam stood frozen in the hallway as students poured from the lunchroom, their cacophony of laughter keeping him in place. He wasn't one of them. He didn't know if he'd ever feel like one of them again.

*Coward.*
*Coward.*
*Coward.*

The word latched on to the synapses in his brain, firing over and over until it was all he heard.

*Coward.*

His gaze lingered on the end of the hall where Peyton stood, her face hidden behind the door of her locker. When his parents first told him he couldn't come home all those months ago, he'd been relieved. He hadn't been ready to face the town, face Peyton.

His best friend needed him, and he'd abandoned her.

As time went on, the training and rehab hardened both his body and his mind. He'd been taught to ignore the pain constantly rocketing up his leg. But that hadn't been the only feeling he'd learned to avoid.

Being away got easier until the distance gave him a sense of peace, a sense of calm. The best way to keep from having to face everything he'd lost was to stay away.

When his trainer told him there was nothing more they could do to help him, his mother allowed him to return home. The facility he'd lived at for eighteen months was never meant to house anyone indefinitely. Especially when the athlete no longer had the promise they'd known him for.

Cameron Tucker had once been meant for greatness.

He hitched his bag higher on his shoulder and ducked around a group of girls congregating outside a classroom.

"I'm not a coward," he mumbled to himself as he walked through the atrium and pushed through the heavy glass doors. At least, he didn't want to be. There was only one thing he could do to prove to himself he was better than that.

His leg ached as he walked across the empty lawn of Twin Rivers High. Students weren't allowed outside during the school day. He scanned the parking lot for the rent-a-cop usually on duty, but she wasn't there.

His too-bright car sat near the back. He'd been late for the third time in the first week of school, but he couldn't tell anyone why. He still hadn't managed to streamline his mornings. Before leaving the training facility, they'd fitted him for a new leg, one that could be covered completely by any pair of pants. It even had a foot that looked real if you didn't peer too closely.

It didn't have the same functionality for running as blade runners, but at the time, he'd been faced with the prospect of seeing everyone he'd left behind. Being able to hide the extent of his injury seemed more important.

Pulling his bag from his shoulder, Cam unzipped it and fished around for his keys. As soon as he found them, he used the electronic fob to unlock the doors and wasted no time in climbing into the back seat.

Peyton's box sat in the carpeted foot well as it had since the day he got the car. Cam ran a hand over the smooth wood, letting his fingers drift under the latch.

*Not a coward.*

*Not a coward.*

The repeated phrase replaced Peyton's words in his mind. He lifted the lid.

Three bulging envelopes rested in the unfinished oak interior. Each was labeled. He read them aloud. "You. Me. Us."

A note sat below the envelopes. He pulled it free, recognizing Peyton's familiar scrawl. A smile tilted his lips.

As he read the note, he could almost hear Peyton's voice in his mind.

---

*If you're reading this, I've already admitted how I feel about you. I hope you don't hate me. Please don't hate me. You're my best friend. I know you don't feel the same way, but we've always been honest with each other.*

---

She'd been wrong. He had felt the same way when he'd kissed her that night. But she'd written the note before that. He rubbed his eyes, willing away the images of her in that tree fort, her cheeks red from the cold.

---

*You probably think this present is stupid, but it was this or some dumb tie, and I've never seen you wear a tie. Oh my gosh, I should have gotten the tie, right?*

*Well, I'm sorry, but I spent weeks on this, so no turning back now.*

*You're going to do amazing things, Cameron Tucker, but only if you believe it as much as I do. That's what this present is about. Whenever you're down or fighting with your dad, when you get a bad running time or lose a sponsorship, read one of the notes in these envelopes.*

*There are three kinds.*

*You: These are the things I think you need reminded of about yourself and what you can do.*

*Me: These are the things I love about you.*

*Us: I just want to make you smile with our favorite jokes or memories.*

*That's it, I guess.*

*Again, please don't hate me. I can take it if you don't have feelings for me, but I can't take losing you.*

*Love, Pey.*

---

Cam's hands shook as he folded the letter once more. *I can't take losing you.* Yet she had. But she wasn't the only one. Cameron Tucker lost himself.

And he didn't know if he could ever return.

He reached for the envelope with "You" written across the front. Inside were many tiny slips of paper. Each said something different.

"Just one," he whispered to himself. He wanted to prove he could face everything he should have confronted eighteen months ago, but it wouldn't happen all at once. Baby steps.

He held the slip out in front of him. The words jumped on the paper until his vision cleared and the words hit him.

---

*Behind all the stress of the competition and your crazy dad, remember this: above all, you love to run.*

---

He closed his eyes, picturing himself in the last meet he'd ever competed in. The feel of the icy wind slapping him in the face. The vibrations racing up his legs with each step. When he ran, he never saw the finish line until he was there. At least, that was how it used to be, before the Olympics became a possibility. Before his father, a failed Olympic hopeful himself, took over Cam's training.

Even after the accident, he'd rehabbed and trained at an Olympic facility. Everyone present was there for one reason: to win.

While getting used to the new leg, running only brought pain. Eventually, Cam stopped associating it with anything good. It was only something that had been taken from him.

The final bell rang, signaling Cam was once again late for

class. He slid from the car and slammed the door, the slip of paper still clutched in his hands.

Shoving it in his pocket, he re-entered the school.

By the time his last class was over, Cam had read Peyton's words more times than he could count. He wouldn't remember a single thing taught in class that afternoon, but it didn't matter.

*Above all, you love to run.*

He did. Once upon a time, he'd loved it. It was a part of him.

He stepped into the locker room and changed into a pair of sweats he'd insisted on wearing for gym—despite the teacher's protests. There was no way he'd have worn shorts.

He left his bag inside, but he took the note from his pocket and stretched it flat against his palm as he walked outside and around the corner of the field house. The track sat like a beacon, calling to him with its chaos.

That was what running was to him. Complete and utter chaos. Pounding hearts. Dripping sweat. Thundering feet. The din blocked out everything else.

He'd been wrong when he thought he wanted the peace distance brought. He'd never been made for calm.

He opened the gate in the chain-link fence and crossed the grassy area next to the long jump pit to where the bleachers shone in the sun. He propped his false foot up on the bottom step, making sure his balance would hold, and began his stretches.

Once he felt loose, he stepped onto the spongy track. A few football players had already made it to the field in the center of the track, but Cam barely noticed them as he set his feet against the familiar white line of the starting point.

He could hear the announcers in his head. *Cameron*

*Tucker, Twin Rivers own running superstar, makes his way around the curve, letting the pack envelope him before making his move. The entire state has been behind this young man, and we expect big things from him.*

During his first few weeks of rehab, Cam had watched his most recent meet incessantly. He'd been unable to grasp the simple fact that it was over, gone in the space of a single night.

But now, all these months later, as he stood on the same starting line he'd known for years, preparing to run the familiar course, the announcer's voice faded away, and it was just him.

He bent forward, inhaling as he prepared for the chaos he craved. He closed his eyes for a moment. When he opened them, all he saw was the path in front of him. As if a starting horn blasted through his mind, he jolted forward, his feet crashing into the lane.

Pain seared up his thigh from where his prosthetic connected, but it only increased the havoc he'd wanted. Anything could happen out on a track. Nothing occurred the same way twice. There were no predictions, no assumptions.

Cam curled into the turn, his heart pounding like a jackhammer trying to crack his chest.

And it only served as a reminder that his heart was still there. He'd often wondered if he'd lost the ability to enjoy anything anymore. Maybe his heart had drifted to the bottom of Defiance Falls in the crash.

But there it was.

*Above all, you love to run.*

A cool breeze blew the hair from his forehead. As he powered down the straightaway, his eyes found familiar blue orbs. She didn't smile or acknowledge him, but she continued to watch him.

He didn't know what she saw. Did she wonder why his speed was so diminished? Did she see that his stride was out of balance or that he needed to use more force to push off his false foot?

He shook his head and kept going, turning his back to her. He may have loved the chaos of running, but Peyton brought that chaos into every other part of his life.

One step at a time.

He let the running soothe him, take him to a place where everything was as it had been when he was a kid. His parents loved him as nothing more than a child, not their ticket to fame. His friendship with Peyton had been so simple, so easy.

His running began in her backyard, racing the twins to impress her. Julian hadn't been very good, but Coop always gave him a challenge. Then they'd laugh and go steal Mrs. Callahan's cupcakes to bring to Peyton.

By the time he stopped running, Peyton was gone. The football team had finished their drills. Members of the track team passed Cam but didn't acknowledge him. He'd never been close with them, seeing them only as competition, never friends.

He'd been single-minded in his pursuit of the Olympics. Basically, an idiot.

But there was one girl who'd always seen through him. "Cameron Tucker." Her voice made him smile despite the exhaustion in his bones.

He turned to find Cara Jasper with her hands on her tiny hips. Daughter of the track coach, she'd always kept a close eye on him.

"Hey, Care Bear." His smile widened.

She crossed her arms. "Don't you 'Care Bear' me. Where have you been?" She hesitated for a moment. "Jerk."

Cam shook his head. Cara was a ten-year-old dictator. Her mother homeschooled her, and she never missed one of her father's track practices. Cam's eyes took her in from her familiar springy blond curls to her small frame and the wheelchair that held it up.

When he didn't respond, she unfolded her arms and gripped her wheels, pushing them toward him. "Where have you been?"

It wasn't the first time he'd been asked the question, nor would it be the last, but it still sent a chill through him. If anyone could understand, it would be Cara. Three years before, she'd been in a car accident and had her spine crushed, an injury she never fully recovered from. She was paralyzed from the waist down.

But if there was something worse than the embarrassment, Cam knew it would be the sympathy he'd get. His parents might be uncaring jerks, but at least they didn't pretend. They never told him it would get better or that life would ever go back to normal.

Cam rubbed the back of his neck. "Ah...my dad sent me to a training facility."

She nodded as if that wasn't a surprise at all. He was Cameron Tucker, after all. State running phenom.

"I was worried about you after..." She didn't voice it, but he knew what two words came next. The accident.

Cam ruffled her hair. "Ah, kiddo, I'm fine." He pasted on a fake smile.

She narrowed her eyes and swatted his hand away. "Are you coming back to the team?"

"I…" He blew out a breath. He hadn't been ready for that question. He loved running. He loved being a part of something. But the team? Competing? The Olympics weren't an option anymore. Didn't that mean he was done?

Cara nodded as if she understood his hesitation. "I get it. You're on a different track than the rest of the team now. You probably have too much training to do to hang around a bunch of mediocre runners. You're too good for us now."

"Cara—" he protested, but she cut him off.

"Gotcha." She grinned. "Well, I'm glad you're back. I know my dad would want you on the team, but you do you. 'Kay, dude?" She held out her fist.

Cam couldn't help the laugh that escaped. "Okay." He bumped his fist to hers. She wheeled herself away, shooting him one final smirk over her shoulder.

He shook his head and stopped at the drinking fountain inside the field house. A group of footballers exited the locker room as he looked up and wiped water from his lips.

Cam pushed into the locker room, stopping short when the only person present turned. Avery. It seemed it would be a day of people he'd left behind. At least Cara spoke to him as if nothing had changed.

Cam went straight to his locker and pulled out his bag without saying a word. He waited for Avery to leave as his friends had, but the other boy just stood frozen in the middle of the smelly room.

Ignoring him, Cam stuffed his jeans into his bag. He couldn't change with Avery in the room. He slung his bag onto his shoulder and stepped past Avery. Before he could escape the charged room, Avery finally spoke.

"You shouldn't have come back."

Cam straightened his spine and turned. He peered at the

boy who'd been his friend and didn't recognize the wild look in his eyes. Cam's leg itched, but he wouldn't give Avery the satisfaction of seeing what the accident had done to him. It destroyed all of them. Did Cam have the same ghosts in his eyes he now saw in Avery's?

"Avery…" He scratched the back of his neck.

Avery shook his head, his jaw flexing. "Why are you here, Cam? We don't want you. This town… what you did to us…"

Cam stepped back. What he did to them? "Avery, I don't understand."

Avery's eyes blazed. "The accident," he spat. "You were driving." He breathed out through his nose. "You killed Cooper."

Cam stumbled back until he hit the bench in front of the lockers. He sank down. "Avery, I wasn't—"

"I don't want to hear your excuses!" He ran a hand through his brown hair, pulling at the ends. "We shouldn't have been in that car. You shouldn't have been driving. This is a warning. Don't cross us. Those of us on the football team, Coop's team, will never forget what you did. Keep your distance, and just maybe, we won't pound your face into the dirt." He turned and stormed from the room before Cam could get another word in.

Cam bent forward, letting his face sink into his hands. Images from that night flickered like a movie, telling the story of the tragedy of Cooper Callahan. But Cam hadn't been behind the wheel.

*"Coop, slow down." Cam leaned between the front seats, trying to make Cooper hear him over the thumping music.*

*Cooper's foot sank down on the gas, and the car lurched forward. They whipped around icy curves, the car fishtailing.*

*"Coop!" Cam latched onto his friend's arm before glancing sideways. "Avery, talk some sense into him."*

*Avery only slouched lower on the seat as his eyes slid closed, and his body heaved again. He mumbled something unintelligible. How much had the two of them drank at the party?*

*"Coop, you need to slow down before we reach the bridge."*

*Cooper shook his head. "My brother is following us. We need to lose him."*

Cam lifted his face as other athletes flooded the room. He stood, grabbed his bag, and walked out into the late afternoon sun. He thought of everything Avery had said about the accident, and the truth struck him in full force.

Avery St. Germaine didn't remember that night. He didn't see images of a dead friend in the spaces of his mind. There was no guilt for anything that happened because he didn't know.

He hadn't seen Julian desperately trying to save his twin in the moments before the car plunged over the falls. He didn't know what the drop felt like. There was no moment in his mind where he knew with clear certainty he was going to die only to wake up days later.

Was Avery the lucky one?

Or did the blank screen of that night hold a different kind of pain?

# Chapter Seven

## PEYTON

~ *Peyton,*

    *I'm sorry about that night.*

    *I'm sorry I kissed you and started whatever this was supposed to be.*

    *But you have got to forget about me.*

    *Cam ~*

"Ugh, are you the only waitress who works at this awful diner?" Addison looked up from her menu.

"Well, you're sitting in my section." Peyton shrugged. "The counter has been my section on this same shift for, like, three years. You're welcome to sit here or anywhere else." She stood, waiting for Addison to make up her mind. It wasn't often Addison came into the diner alone. It wasn't often she did anything alone.

"Whatever, I'm waiting on some friends." Addison waved her away.

"Sure, you just let me know when you and your friends are ready to order from this awful diner." Peyton went back to filling the salt and pepper shakers at the waitress station behind the counter.

"Really, honey?" Peyton's mom whispered. "What was that? You two used to be inseparable."

"We used to be a lot of things, Mom."

"Oh honey, losing Cooper was hard on everyone. Especially those who loved him and knew him the way you and your friends did. He'd be crushed to see you all scattered to the winds now."

Julian gave a disgusted snort as he rushed past them to bus tables to make room for the growing crowd.

"I think it's hardest for Julian." She shook her head. "That one still has a lot of anger he's not dealing with yet."

"It's Julian, Mom. When is he ever not angry?"

"I know it's hard, Peyton, but he needs you. Honestly, you two need each other. Try to be a little more understanding."

Peyton nodded. In theory, her mom was probably right. But in reality, Coop and Julian had never gotten along. The twins were like oil and water. Unless that was what had Julian in such a foul mood since his return. Maybe he was feeling all kinds of guilt for hating his brother all those years?

A crash of breaking dishes and clattering silverware pulled Peyton out of her thoughts.

"Watch where you're going!" Addison's shrill voice rang out across the noisy diner.

Peyton looked up to see Julian trying to help Addison up

from the pile of dirty dishes and the slop of leftover food on the floor.

Peyton suppressed a laugh when Addie slipped and fell again.

"Easy now, I got you." Julian said, taking her by the arms and pulling her to her feet. He held her close, trying to keep her from slipping again. She stared at him for a moment in surprise—the way people often did when they confused him with Cooper.

"No." She struggled to move away from him, slipping and falling once again in the mess.

"It's okay, Addie." Julian crouched beside her.

"No. Get away from me!" She scrambled across the floor, smearing ranch dressing across her red dress.

Peyton frowned, stepping out from behind the counter. Something wasn't right. She knew Addison Parker better than most people. She wasn't mad or embarrassed. Addie was…scared.

"Let me help you, Addie," Julian said, taking another step toward her.

"Don't touch me." Her voice shook as she threw her hands up in front of her face as if to protect herself.

"Hey, Addison," Julian said. "Look at me." He crouched down beside her. "Look at my eyes. See? One brown and one blue. I'm not him."

He sat next to her, careful not to touch her as she took a deep breath. Her hands fell back to her lap.

"Right," she whispered. "Julian."

"Sorry I ran into you with this crap. Send us your dry-cleaning bill." He made light of the stressful moment as he got Addison back on her feet and away from the slippery mess.

The moment she looked up to the sea of faces watching their exchange, Addie's face flushed bright red, and she bolted for the door.

Julian took a step to follow her.

"Don't," Peyton called as she grabbed Addie's purse and keys from her seat at the counter and followed her out the door.

*Why on earth would Addison Parker be afraid of Julian?*

"What was that?" Peyton jogged across the parking lot to where Addison leaned against her car.

"Nothing." Addison straightened, wiping her eyes.

"Addie, are you okay?" Peyton's voice softened.

"Fine," she snapped.

"What happened to us, Addison? We used to be friends?"

"*Friends?* Addison glared at her. "Friends don't abandon their friends when they need them the most." She snatched her purse and keys from Peyton's hands. "*Friends* don't let a stupid guy eclipse everything else going on around them."

"What are you talking about?"

"You! You were so wrapped up in your own little world that night…" She shook her head in disgust. "A lot of people have failed me in my life, Peyton. I just never thought you'd be one of them." She stepped into her car and slammed the door, leaving Peyton bewildered.

*"Oh my gosh! They're here. They're here!"* Addison's voice hit a piercing note, making Peyton cringe.

*"Calm down, girl. You're trying to play it cool, remember. We don't care if the cheerleaders show up to your party or not."* Peyton

adjusted the adorable string of Christmas lights woven into Addie's hair.

"Right." Addison nodded.

"Go hang out with Coop," Nari suggested. "They're all half in love with him even if they won't admit it. It'll impress them to know you hang with him and some of the guys from the team."

"Good idea. I'll see you girls later." She turned to go but whirled back around. "Peyton Lillian Callahan, why aren't you off seducing Cameron?"

"Julian crashed our date when he hitched a ride with us, and it was weird when we got here. He's off with Avery now."

"Ugh, Julian's such a jerk. I didn't even invite him."

"You know he doesn't care about stuff like that," Nari said, frowning at the way Addison swayed on her feet as she took another sip of her drink. "You should slow down, Addie." She took the cup from her friend. "The party is just getting started."

"I didn't eat anything today, so it's hitting me harder than usual." Addie ran her hand over her clammy brow.

"Go find Coop and tell him to feed you," Peyton said. "I'm going to find Cam and get this date back on track."

"Look for the mistletoe!" Addison called. "I hung them everywhere!" Addie stumbled, clutching Nari for support.

"Thanks." Peyton waved. "Don't be such a lightweight, Addie! Go find a sandwich or something with actual carbs."

Peyton shook her head, mopping up the mess Julian had made when he ran right into Addison heading for the bathroom.

*It doesn't make sense.* Nothing about that Christmas Eve

party more than a year ago accounted for Addison's behavior just now.

*How did I fail her?* Addie was just as excited about finally getting Peyton and Cameron under the mistletoe as Peyton was. She'd hung the stuff everywhere just for them.

"How can I fix something when I don't even know what's broken?"

# Chapter Eight

## CAMERON

~ Cam,

*I know you're better than they think you are.*

*Peyton ~*

"No," Cam groaned. Water filled his lungs as he struggled to break the surface. His left leg had gone numb before the water even pushed him over the falls. He sucked in a breath as his head emerged from the frothing water.

Cam's eyes snapped open, and he bolted upright, the blanket falling from around his waist.

"Cam, honey. You're okay." His mother sat at the end of his bed.

Her voice didn't calm him as a mother's should. As it once had. He slid back until he rested against his headboard. His pillow had fallen to the floor at some point during the night.

He never remembered the exact dreams, but the ice they left in his veins remained.

"Cam," his mother tried again. "When was the last time you slept through the night?" Cecilia Tucker liked to believe she took care of him. She liked to think he needed her. But over the years, her fitness empire left little time for unimportant family life.

The day after the accident, she'd gone back to work making her celebrity fitness videos and letting his father arrange to send Cam away from home.

Her eyes scanned his face for only a moment before traveling down to where his stump now lay uncovered. Her eyes widened only a fraction, just enough for the anger in Cam to bubble to the surface. Eighteen months later and now his deformity surprised her?

The psychologist they had made him see at the training center would have chastised him for the term deformity. She always told him his loss didn't make him weaker or less than but only unique.

Everyone had their own set of challenges, she'd say. This was his.

He yanked the blanket back over himself and met her sorrowful gaze. He had no illusions that her sorrow was for him. She hated what she'd lost. There was a time when their family was on the rise. She was the fitness guru who had a son destined for the Olympics and a husband who'd get him there.

"Cam." She sighed, moving past the awkwardness. "Your father and I need to speak with you. Please come downstairs." Without another word, she rose, flattened the creases in her dress pants, and left the room.

Cam leaned his head back, lifting his eyes to the stars

above. He shifted sideways and scooted his legs over the edge of the bed.

Peyton's wooden box sat on the table beside it. He'd brought it in from the car for the first time, thinking it would help chase away the darkness in his mind.

But some darkness was absolute.

He rubbed his tired eyes and leaned down, reaching for the silicone socket that sometimes felt like it had become part of him. He rolled it on, taking his time, before grabbing the prosthetic and aligning it with the pin before pulling it up. All the air from the socket left almost like it had been placed in a vacuum.

When Cam first started training how to walk with the prosthetic, the limb had felt foreign on his body. Now, it was as if it had always been there. For him, at least. The people of Twin Rivers wouldn't see it that way.

He pushed himself from the bed and managed to get dressed without falling like he still sometimes did.

Down in the kitchen, his parents sat at the small white table, waiting for him. Matching timid expressions greeted him.

His smoothie sat ready on the counter, but he didn't touch it. Instead, he went to the cabinet and pulled out the box of pop tarts he hadn't bothered to hide. When he was training for the Olympics, he'd never imagined himself indulging in sugar and carbs. Now, he didn't care. If he was going to sit down with his parents, he'd need the boost.

His father drummed his fingers on the table as Cam sat. His mother shifted her eyes away, unable to look at him after seeing his stump.

Fine. He bit into his pop tart. His father scowled.

"Cameron, you shouldn't eat such things if you're going to train."

Cam almost choked on his food. He swallowed. "Excuse me? Train?" He did realize what had happened to him, right? Even the coaches at the center couldn't get him to a point where he'd had any hope of succeeding. That was why they sent him home after so long.

His father sighed as if the answer was obvious. "Coach Jasper told me you've been running on the school track. I don't know why you didn't tell me."

One time. He'd been to the track once, and word reached his father. "Unbelievable." He tried to push back from the table, but his father gripped the back of his chair.

"You will stay until we're finished."

Cam shook his head but didn't try to leave again. Allen Tucker never backed down until he got his way. At least, not anymore. He'd once been like Cam, an Olympic hopeful with big dreams. Cam's dreams had been crushed through no fault of his own, but his father lost his chance by making the wrong choices. The name Allen Tucker became synonymous with performance-enhancing drugs. He'd spent every moment since then trying to get back to the show. For a while, Cam was his ticket.

His father was quiet for a moment before uttering one word. "Paralympics."

Cam sat back, the full force of the word striking him in the chest. His father had always claimed the Paralympics weren't a real competition. He'd been wrong. Those men and women earned every one of their medals. They were the strongest athletes in the world.

But Cam's father was a jerk.

Cam considered his next words carefully. "I've tried this,

Dad. For eighteen months, you sent me across the country to a training facility. It. Did. Not. Help."

Cam's mother placed a hand on his arm. "We didn't send you, dear. You needed time to recover away from this place. You chose to go."

This was too much. If they believed that, they were delusional. His parents paid a lot of money for him to spend so long there. His father pulled in favors to keep him there after he refused to train for months on end.

He'd even sent a threatening letter to Cam when he heard Cam wouldn't run once his rehab was complete. That was when the psychologist visits began. Eventually, he'd started running again. But he'd refused to change his prosthetic once he'd gotten used to it. He hadn't cared that others would allow him to increase his speed.

"We need to get you blades." His father's voice cut through his self-pitying inner argument.

He snapped his head up, meeting the stern eyes of his father, his coach. "No."

His father rose from his chair, towering over the table. "What do you mean, no?"

Cam stood to face him. "I don't want to do it anymore. I'm done competing."

"I didn't raise a quitter, boy!" Red veins snaked up his father's neck.

"No, you raised a machine and then threw me away when I broke. Let me ask you something, Dad. I've been training to make it to the Olympics for years. Have you ever once wondered if I wanted to do it? Did you even consider that a teenage boy might not want to wake up at five AM every morning? He might want to be able to keep friends without feeling like it was only a distraction?" He glanced from his father to his open-mouthed mother. "That he might have wanted to recover from the worst night of his life surrounded by his family instead of a bunch of therapists at some unfamiliar clinical rehab facility."

Cam stepped back from the table. "When I left here, I'd lost everything, but I was still me. Still Cam. Do you want to know what eighteen months of pain and strangers and abandonment did to me? Just look. Do you see your son standing before you." He turned his back on them, shaking his head. "I didn't think so."

He climbed the stairs to his room and stuffed a pair of sweats and a T-shirt in a duffle before sliding in Peyton's box. He couldn't be in his house for a moment longer. At least tonight.

After he grabbed his keys and opened the front door, he froze. A man stood on the doorstep, lifting his hand to knock. Cam scanned his ill-fitting suit and too-charming grin.

"Cameron Tucker." He stuck out his hand.

Cam only glared at it. This was just perfect. He could spot a reporter anywhere.

The man dropped his hand, seemingly unfazed. "I'm here to talk to you about your return to the Olympic chatter."

Cam glanced back over his shoulder to where his father now stood in the entryway. "Talk to him."

He pushed past him and hurried to his car before anyone could stop him. Tossing his bag in the back seat, he climbed in.

He needed to see the one person who'd understand. The one person he'd pushed away.

*You're a coward.*

He had been. He'd given everything he could to his father.

He'd let him try to live his dreams through his son. Cam didn't know what lay in his future, but he couldn't go back to training. Not yet. Not when there were other pieces of himself he had to find first.

*Above all, you love to run.*

And training stole that love. He wanted it back.

A few minutes later, he pulled up in front of the house that had felt more like home than his own. Peyton might be mad at him, hurt, but she'd never turn him away. Not when he needed her.

He breathed deeply and opened the door. The front lawn leading up to the large red-brick house was manicured to perfection. Flowering bushes sat along the front underneath large bay windows. He forced himself to keep walking despite the nerves in his stomach.

His fingers gripped the cold bronze knocker. Before he could stop himself, he knocked it against the door three times.

At first, no one came. He was about to turn around in defeat when the door swung open and Cooper's face greeted him.

His breath came out in short pants until his mind cleared. Not Cooper. Julian.

Julian's eyes held the only bit of emotion he showed. Shock. Did he want Cam to leave? He probably did.

An image of Julian on the hood of the car, crowbar in hand, knocked the air from Cam's lungs. He shook his head and met the other boy's eyes. As he peered closer, he could see little changes. His face had lost any bit of softness he'd once had. Dark stubble coated his jaw.

But it was the way he held himself that spoke of every-thing they'd been through. Julian had always had a carefree grace about him. Both twins had. Now, his posture was stiff, almost as if he considered each movement before making it.

"Cam," he finally said, his voice gruff as if he'd only just woken up.

"Julian."

They stared at each other a moment longer before Julian finally sighed. "What are you doing here?"

That was a good question. Suddenly, Cam didn't know anymore. He hadn't been friends with Julian since they were kids, but they'd spent a considerable amount of time together with Peyton and Coop. Yet, seeing Julian felt like looking at himself. The same grief he'd been carrying reflected back at him.

No one else knew what it had felt like to be in that car. No one except Cam and Julian. Avery didn't remember. Cooper was gone.

Cam rubbed the back of his neck. "I...uh..."

"Cameron?" Mrs. Callahan appeared behind Julian and slapped him on the back of the head. "Why didn't you invite him in?" She turned her kind eyes on Cam. The kind of look Peyton always hated because she felt her mother approved of Cam more than she did her own daughter.

"Cam, honey." She smiled. "Why don't you come in? Peyton is in the shower, but you're welcome to wait for her." She pushed Julian out of the way. "We've missed you around here."

He couldn't do it. He couldn't cross that threshold while she stared at him expectantly. He took a step back.

"Mom," Julian grumbled. "Leave him alone."

Mrs. Callahan frowned. "Julian, weren't you practicing your guitar?"

He took the hint and threw his hands up in surrender before walking away.

"I'm sorry, Mrs. Callahan." Cam stumbled back. "This was a mistake." He turned, mumbling to himself. "Everything was a mistake."

She watched him get into his car, and she was still there when he drove away.

Cam slammed the door of his car and walked toward the hill that sloped down to the falls. He clutched Peyton's box under one arm as he tried to descend to where the rushing water crashed against the rocks. He'd been to the river since returning to Twin Rivers, but he'd avoided Defiance Falls.

But no matter how far away he stayed, it never left his mind. In the distance, the bridge shone in the sun. Concrete pylons rose up to embrace the busy road as it meandered over the water.

He averted his eyes, choosing instead to focus on his footing. He'd grown used to the prosthetic over the months, but some skills were still a struggle. Going downhill, for one.

His toe hit the grass, sending him pitching forward. The box crashed to the ground, but someone gripped his arm before he could follow it.

He released a breath and steadied himself before glancing down to make sure his leg was still covered. Satisfied, he finally glanced at the person who'd save him from tumbling down to the path at the bottom of the hill.

Nari released him with a smile, her eyes crinkling behind the thick frames of her glasses. "Hey." She stuck her hands in the pockets of her jean shorts and kicked her toe against the ground.

Cam hadn't expected company at the falls, but only a cold-hearted person could turn Nari away. As shy as she was, she was still one of the nicest girls in their school.

When he didn't respond, she raised an eyebrow and bent to pick up the box he'd dropped. "Are these the notes Peyton gave you that night?" No one who'd been there needed to ask which night she was referring to.

Some of the notes had spilled on the ground. One lifted into the air as the breeze struck it. Nari jumped forward and snatched it before it blew away. She stared at the note and then jerked her hand toward him. "I'm sorry. I shouldn't have read that."

Cam hesitated before taking the note. It wasn't until his eyes fell to the words that he knew which of Peyton's envelopes it had come from.

---

*I know you better than they do.*

---

It was a "me" note with an arrow at the bottom. He flipped the slip of paper over.

---

*I know you're better than they think you are. You're my best friend, Cameron Tucker.*

---

She was wrong. He wasn't any different from his parents.

They'd abandoned him after the accident by sending him away. He'd abandoned Peyton by leaving without a word.

He opened the box and stuck the note inside before slamming the lid and tossing it onto the grass. She'd given him the present when she thought her words would help him through everything. When she knew him better than anyone else.

He brushed the hair from his eyes and focused on the churning falls. It was strange how the worst day of his life happened right there, yet he felt a kinship to the thrashing water. It never calmed, never settled. It was as if it took hold of him that night and continued to rage inside him.

Nari stood silently next to him. Cam could have forgotten she was even there if he didn't crave company so much. Her presence was a welcome distraction. For all the time he'd spent alone over the past year, he'd never felt the crushing weight of loneliness. Not until returning to Twin Rivers. Not until he tried to step back into his old life only to feel his own absence. Like he was a shadow, desperately trying to grasp onto something, anything familiar, before fading away.

Cam descended the rest of the way down the hill to where the walking path meandered by the falls, sloping up toward where the two rivers converged on the north side of the bridge.

A rail divided the walking paths from the flowing water. That hadn't been there before. Neither had the warning signs marking the edge of the water.

As if reading his thoughts, Nari spoke. "They put those up after the accident."

"But this isn't where the accident took place." He lifted his eyes in the direction of the bridge though he couldn't see it from where he stood.

"There's a sign on the bridge too, but they put more up when there's ice."

Cam nodded. Ice. Right. Because the bridge wasn't a dangerous part of the road, not normally. The road leading to it curved and wound down alongside the river, but the speed slowed as you reached the crossing. That night, the bridge became deadly, but it wasn't through any fault other than the boys in that car.

Cam released a breath and sat on the bench near the rail, leaning forward with his elbows resting on his knees.

Nari set the box aside for a second time and took a seat beside him.

"How did you know I'd be here?" Cam asked.

Nari pulled her long ebony hair over one shoulder and tucked her hands under her thighs. "I didn't." She chewed on her lip for a moment of hesitation. "I was pulling up to Peyton's as you were leaving, so I followed you."

Cam lifted a brow and peered sideways at her. "Why?"

"Why?" Confusion flickered across her face.

"Yeah, why? You seem to be the only person in this stupid town who doesn't stare at me every time I'm near."

"Maybe I just don't find you all that pleasant to look at." She pressed her lips together to suppress a smile.

Cam shook his head, the beginnings of a genuine smile tilting his lips. He'd almost forgotten what that felt like. "You talk to me as if nothing has changed. I don't understand. It seems like everyone else wishes I'd just stayed gone so I didn't have to come home and remind them of what happened."

Nari's smile fell. "If by everyone you mean Peyton, you

have to cut her some slack. You're not the only one who suddenly returned. Julian is back, and believe me, if you think you have issues in this town, you don't know the half of it. You'll eventually move on, eventually get over the accident. But Julian... He has to see Cooper every time he looks in the mirror. Peyton has to see him every time she's near Julian. And their parents..." She shook her head. "It's been eighteen months, Cam, but this town still hurts."

Cam rubbed the metal of his leg through his pants. Nari didn't know that he too had a constant reminder.

Nari sighed. "Pey was doing okay. Sort of. None of this has been easy for her." She poked his side. "And you coming back only made it harder."

He rubbed a hand over his face. "I know. But I just can't..." He shook his head.

Nari was quiet for a moment. "Why aren't you running?"

He shrugged, but Nari didn't let that be enough.

"Everyone thought you were back to take the track team to state one final time before joining the Olympic team. Or at least trying to make it. You've spent the last eighteen months training, haven't you? Why stop now?"

Cam lifted his head to look at her. "Nari, just say what I know you truly want to say." Nari didn't know the entire truth, but she knew more than anyone else. She'd sent Cam letters every month. He didn't know how she'd pried the address out of his mom, and he'd hated receiving anything from home. At first. But she spoke mostly of Peyton, and it helped him get through everything.

But, it meant she knew the kind of facility he'd been in. Training, yes, but also rehabilitation. And the look she gave him said she knew more than she'd let on.

He rubbed the back of his neck and let his eyes drift to the water again. "You know."

She nodded. "I haven't told anyone if that's what you're worried about." Her words came rapidly. "Peyton was having a really hard time, so I wanted to figure out when you were coming home. I went to your house and found your mother...drunk."

Cam snapped his eyes to hers. "My mother doesn't get drunk." She'd always been so careful with her image, saying letting alcohol control one's actions was sloppy and undignified.

Nari shrugged. "She missed you."

He shook his head. Another thing that didn't sound like his mother. "When was this?"

"A few months after the accident. She answered the door, and I knew something was off right away. Your father wasn't home. I called Peyton, and she came. We got your mom to bed and then stayed to make sure she was okay. Peyton stayed the entire night, but as I was leaving, I found something on the table by the door. It had tears soaked into the page, and I wanted to see what it was that could make a woman like your mom break down."

She brought her hands into her lap and wrung them together. "My mother always tells me I'm too nosy for my own good." She laughed nervously. "But it had your name on it. I just wanted to help your mom and help Peyton."

"Nari." Cam clenched the edges of the bench. "Spit it out."

"It was a progress report from a physical therapist. That's how I got the center's address. They detailed how you were doing with your...prosthetic."

Cam closed his eyes, waiting for the feeling of shame to go away. A pressure on his hand made him opened his eyes.

He didn't know what he expected to see in Nari. Pity? Was that why she was the only person who accepted him back into her life? The only one who didn't make him work for it?

"I think you should tell her."

It took a moment for Nari's words to register in his mind. He stood and turned away to pace toward the rail. "Why didn't you?"

"Because it would hurt her to hear it from anyone other than you."

Cam turned. "Hurt her? I'm missing a leg, Nari. How does that hurt her?"

Nari stood, uncharacteristic anger rising in her eyes. "So what?"

He clenched his jaw. "I think you should go."

She crossed her arms. "Peyton is my friend. I won't leave until I've said what needs to be said."

"And what exactly is that?"

"I'm sorry you were injured, Cam. I am. It sucks. I'm sorry your parents are dicks and that your homecoming has been...not great. But you know what? It's a leg. Just flesh. You got a replacement. And running... I know you could still do it if you wanted. You lost your dream. Again, so what? None of that matters!" She sighed, the tension leaving her shoulders.

"We are what matters. Not our legs or any other physical thing we could lose. Pey lost herself when Coop died and Julian left. She lost you. That's worse than any leg. I've watched that girl be in love with you the entire time I've known her. And yet, you've made her feel unlovable." A tear slid down her cheek. "How could you do that, Cam? After everything that's been taken from you, how could you give away the one thing that was irreplaceable?"

She turned to trudge back up the hill and paused. "Peyton won't care about the leg, Cam. It doesn't make you damaged. It doesn't change who you were before. I hope you can find him, the Cam we all knew. When you do, please bring Peyton back to us. We all need her. Not everyone sees that. Coop is gone. Julian is...something else. Avery blames all of us. And Addison... Something happened to her that night to take her from us too. Peyton is the glue, or the metal, used to fill the holes on our cracked surface. And you... You're the crazy old guy on the beach with a metal detector, trying to find the treasure that's been buried in the sand."

She turned her head to meet his eyes and smirked.

Cam couldn't help his smile. "Crazy old guy on the beach, huh?"

She nodded. "Completely crazy. But you'll find her. You always do." She climbed the rest of the way up the path to her car.

Cam sat back down on the bench, Nari's words rolling around in his mind. She was usually the quietest among them, the self-proclaimed nerd of the group. But maybe she saved her words for just when they needed to hear them. She'd done it before on the night of the accident. She'd said the words that gave him the courage to face his feelings for Peyton.

*It doesn't make you damaged. It doesn't change who you were before.*

He fumbled open Peyton's box, pulling out the envelope marked "Us."

The note he chose was longer than the rest. Peyton's words rolled off the paper, cloaking him in their memories.

*Do you remember when we were kids? We thought nothing could ever hurt us. We were wrong. But every time I hurt, Cam, you're there. No matter what happens, we'll always be there for each other.*

"No matter what happens," he whispered, folding the note and slipping it into his pocket. Nari was right. Cam's leg wouldn't change the way Peyton saw him. She was better than that.

He had to tell her before she found out some other way.

Could he fix them before it was too late?

# Chapter Nine

## PEYTON

~ Peyton,
   You're going to be okay without me. You have to be.
   Cam ~

"Listen to this one," Katie said.

"The pursuit of perfection is an illusion none of us will ever attain. No matter how thin, pretty, or rich we are there will always be something society tells us isn't good enough—something we're supposed to be ashamed about.

Two days ago at lunch, one of my 'friends' said she'd rather kill herself than be fat—and she looked right at me when she said it, like I should take her advice! Luckily I'm strong enough not to care what she says, but there are plenty *of girls out there who would let a comment like that affect them.*

*But you know what's sad? According to my doctor I am at the perfect weight for my height and age. I'm a healthy weight and I have people telling me I should kill myself for being fat? Is that really what our reality is like? Why do we do this to each other?"*

**@Healthy&HappySoLeaveMeAlone**

---

"Yes! That's so perfect," Peyton said. "I need to pull that quote for the project portfolio."

"You're so going to win this scholarship, Peyton," Katie said.

"I can't believe people at our school are really using my app. I kinda thought the initial interest would fade after a few weeks."

"Now that we're back at school, No BS is even more popular." Katie tapped a few more keys on her computer, checking the latest app activity. "I'm kind of obsessed with it myself." She laughed. "I check it all the time."

"I couldn't have done it without you and your mom's help," Peyton said. "I wish I could pay your mom for all the work she's done helping me get the security system in place. No BS would never work if we couldn't guarantee absolute anonymity to our users, or at least work toward that. And I would have fallen flat on my face without your mad coding skills."

"We make a good team," Katie said. "I don't have the creativity to do what you've done with the app. It's really amazing, Peyton. I'm thrilled to be a part of it behind the scenes."

"I wish there was a scholarship in it for you too." Peyton felt bad that Katie had spent so much time volunteering to help with Peyton's summer project when there wasn't much in it for her. The grand prize was a full ride to Peyton's choice of STEM-focused universities. Peyton had a talent for coding, but there were some aspects she was still learning. That was where Katie's mom swooped in and saved the day.

"I'm happy to help. It's so rewarding to see so *many* people dealing with the same issues and coming together on this app to support each other. It's phenomenal."

"It really has opened my eyes in a way I never expected," Peyton admitted. "When I started planning No BS, I had girls like me in mind. The fat girls who never get a voice. Do you know how hard it is to listen to people ridicule a girl with a weight problem and then watch her brush it off like it's no big deal because she's really not *allowed* to defend herself. Girls like me see that harsh judgment in everyone's eyes wherever we go, but our bodies are all anyone ever sees. People don't see my GPA or how I speak two languages and can code circles around our STEM team. They don't see how kind I am or how creative I am. They don't see the things that make me the person I am. All they see is the imperfection I wear for the world to see every day of my life. Other people can hide their imperfections, but fat girls don't get that luxury. So, I made No Body Shame to give them a small community where they could vocalize their deepest hurts and fears to like-minded listeners. But then I discovered this whole other world of secret hurts and shames that we all deal with no matter how big or small, and I realized No BS was for a much larger community."

"I'm glad you opened it to the whole school and not just a beta group." Katie started packing her things. "It's opened my

CURVY GIRLS CAN RULE

eyes too. I always thought I was alone in my struggles. Few people give the weird girl with the odd fashion sense much credit either. I'm easy to mock, and I know it. I used to think I should conform just to get the targets off my back. I tried for a little while in ninth grade, but I hated me, and everyone else was just as indifferent as ever." She shrugged. "So I promised myself that I would just let my freak flag fly and be happy with who I am. Having No BS has shown me there are plenty of other weirdos out there who feel the same way. I've made a few new friends on the app, and we've even met IRL, and it's been great. Your app gave me the kind of friends I never thought I'd have. And that includes you." Katie leaned in to give Peyton a hug. "You deserve whatever good things come from No BS. I can't imagine you won't win. No Body Shame is exactly the kind of online social experiment the competition was made for. You've got this in the bag, Peyton."

"We'll see." Peyton sighed. "The final submissions are due this week, and I'm so nervous!"

"When will you find out if you won?"

"The grand prize will be awarded right before the holi-days." And that was the reason Peyton had entered in the first place. No matter how small her chances were, if she made it all the way, she could count on having a great distraction during the worst time of year for her and her family. And if she actually won, then this time next year she would be far, far away from Twin Rivers and all its bad memories.

"I'll have my fingers crossed for you," Katie said as she left.

Peyton sat at her laptop, engrossed in the No BS comments from the past few days. She attempted to respond to everyone, but the more popular the app got, the harder it was for her to keep up.

Her STEM studies teacher, Mr. Hale, was really impressed with her project and wanted to present it to the state school board after the winners were announced. He thought the app should be available statewide to all public schools. Peyton smiled at the very idea of so many schools participating in something she created.

---

*"I had an argument with my best friend over a stupid dress! She borrowed my favorite dress for a date she was really excited about. But she's way more chesty than I am and accidentally split the bust seam. I was upset, and I called her a fat slut, like just because she has big boobs that automatically makes her a slut? I don't even know why I said that! What's wrong with me? How do I fix this?"*
  **@GirlsBeKindToGirls**

---

*@GirlsBeKindToGirls, Unfortunately us girls have inherited some bad habits from previous generations. Somehow the busty girl is supposed to be the slut and the mean girl has to be mean in order to stay on top of the rest of us, the girl with glasses is always the smarty pants nerd and the cheerleader is the snobby rich girl. It's like we're programmed to think this way and make these snap judgments that have no real basis in truth. We have got to be the generation that stops this madness.*

*If she's really your best friend, she will forgive you. True best friends forgive and forget—no matter what. But you've got to own up to your mistakes and really talk about what you said and why you said it. Talk it out with your friend and then make a No BS pact to never body shame each other again.*

*Best of luck*

**@CupcakesAreMyNemesis, @NoBSmod**

---

Peyton clicked send before her own words really resonated with her. *True best friends forgive and forget—no matter what.* Did that include surviving the death of a brother and the disappearance of said friend? Since his return, Peyton had avoided Cameron as much as possible. Facing him, facing everything that had happened, was just too much. But what kind of friend was she if she didn't give their friendship a chance? Didn't give Cam a chance? She'd gained weight since that night, and she hated herself for it, but the Cameron she knew would never judge her. He was better than that.

# Chapter Ten

## CAMERON

---

~ Cam,

Do you remember when we were kids?
We thought nothing could ever hurt us.
We were wrong.

Peyton ~

---

*Son, we think you need to see a shrink.* Of course, because his father would only use the term that belittles their profession. It was how he operated. The appointment must have been his mother's idea. His father was more of the "man up" kind of guy.

Cam let the appointment card fall into the trash can. He'd seen a psychiatrist during his entire stay at the Emerson facility. They'd claimed it was necessary for his recovery. Maybe it had been, but all he remembered about it was sitting in front of a complete stranger being asked to spill his innermost thoughts. He'd never even been someone who'd shared how he felt with the people he trusted.

He replaced the appointment card that had been in his hand with another one of Peyton's notes.

---

*Potato Pancakes.*

---

Just two words and Peyton could help him forget about another crummy conversation with his parents. *Potato Pancakes.*

During freshman year, Peyton's mother was hospitalized with exhaustion. Peyton's father wouldn't leave the hospital, which meant the diner either had to close or be run by four teenagers.

Mrs. Callahan told them to close the doors and turn customers away. She even called the cook herself and told him not to come in. But, Peyton, being Peyton, decided they could handle it. She enlisted Cam to help her cook while Cooper and Julian waited tables.

It wasn't until they got there that she learned the only thing Cam knew how to cook was a potato pancake recipe his grandma taught him. She didn't panic though. She still trusted him in the kitchen more than her brothers. So, she put out a sign that called it potato pancake day.

The four of them perfected the pancake flip—sending a potato pancake flying from the griddle to a plate held by one of the twins. They were such a hit Mrs. Callahan had them do it again the next year. She also made them clean every inch of that kitchen for disobeying her order to close.

He read the note again. *Potato pancakes.* The memory of the four of them together put a huge smile on his face.

Who needed therapy when they had Peyton?

But he didn't have Peyton. Not quite. He wanted her back, like they used to be. Lazy weekends in the diner. Hanging out by the river. Support. Friendship. How could he have given all of that up?

He shook his head and walked across the track to where his second-favorite girl sat next to the bleachers. He dropped onto the seat beside her and looked over her shoulder at her phone.

"What's up, Care Bear?"

She shoved her phone in her pocket as if he'd caught her doing something she shouldn't be doing. She looked sideways at him. "Cam Jam."

He raised an eyebrow, but she only shrugged. "Trying it out."

"What were you reading?" He nodded to where her phone stuck out of her pocket. It lit up with a new notification.

"Nothing." She spoke too quickly.

For once, Cam wasn't the one hiding something, and he enjoyed the feeling. "Was it a boy, Cara?" He suppressed a grin.

"Ugh. Gross." She screwed up her face. "Like I want to go anywhere near a smelly creature like you." Her cheeks blazed red.

A few months before he left, Coach Jas pulled him aside and told him he worried Cara had a crush. He'd wanted Cam to be careful with her feelings. Coach hadn't needed to worry. Cam wasn't like the other jerks on the team who ignored the kid tagging along. He liked her. But coach had been wrong about the crush. She'd only wanted a friend.

Cam recognized that now because the same loneliness existed in him as well.

He wished he'd seen it at the time.

She studied him for a moment then let out a sigh. "You really want to know?"

He gripped the arm of her wheelchair. "Only if you want to tell me."

She lifted her eyes to the gray afternoon sky. It was only a matter of time before rain overtook their Saturday. "Fine." She pulled her phone free and unlocked the screen before handing it to him.

Cam could feel Coach Jas's eyes on them as they talked. It wasn't unusual for the team to have Saturday practices on off weeks when there wasn't a meet. None of the runners paid them any mind.

His eyes fell onto the logo at the top of the screen. "No BS. What's this?"

"No Body Shame." She clutched her hands in her lap. "It's supposed to only be for the high school but all the kids at the lower school have found a way to download the app."

He scanned the paragraphs of text, each attributed to a different screen name.

---

*Sometimes, when they tell me I should hate the hijab on my head, I believe them.*
   **@BeingDifferentSucks**

---

*Why can't I look like everyone else? Nothing works to stop the breakouts. I don't blame them. I don't want to look at my face either. Their words hurt, but they're nothing I haven't said to myself a thousand times.*

**@HidingInTheShadows**

---

Cam scrunched his brow. "Care Bear." He rubbed the ridge of his nose and scrolled down.

---

*Damaged. That's what they tell me I am. And they're right. I am broken. My body doesn't work the same way as anyone else's. I can't even walk without having trouble. There are times when I can't get a single one of my muscles to work. I fell down a packed stairwell last week. And the sad thing is that isn't even the most embarrassing thing that has happened to me because of this stupid illness.*

**@TheBrokenDoll**

---

When Cam let the phone fall into Cara's lap, she touched his arm.

"How…" He shook his head. "I've never seen this app before."

"It's new. Apparently created by a senior. No one knows who. I heard some of the team talking about it. Everything on it is anonymous. Cam…"

He met her soft brown eyes. "Yeah, Care?"

"Can you tell me the truth?"

"About what?"

She let out an exasperated breath. "About you. You come back after a year and a half and claim to have been training for the Olympics, yet something isn't right. I saw you run. Your gait is off. Most people don't have a near perfect stride, but you did. Something changed that. And you're slow. Like, ungodly slow. The Cam I knew would never have let himself run like crap."

Cam sat back. "You're ten. You shouldn't be able to see all of this."

She tore her eyes from his. "Eleven, actually. You'd know that if you'd been here."

Cara had always been like the little sister Cam never had, and he suddenly needed someone to get him, to know what he was going through, and tell him it was okay to deal with it in his own way. She was a kid but more perceptive than any adult he knew. There was no curiosity in her gaze. She wasn't a gossip who wanted to know the latest news. She was worried.

He pushed himself from the bleachers, feeling Peyton's note still in the palm of his hand. *Potato Pancakes.* A time when he'd been happy, content. He wanted that again, and the first step was telling someone, anyone, what had happened to him. Facing his greatest fear.

"Can you come with me?" he asked.

Cara nodded. "Sure, Cam Jam."

He gripped the handles of her wheelchair and pushed her around the side of the bleachers where they wouldn't be seen by those on the track. He stopped and turned her to face him.

"This isn't a very good abduction," she smirked. "You aren't supposed to stop."

"Cara…" He choked out her name as fear seized him. He couldn't do it. He couldn't show her. His mind drifted back to the app she'd shown him full of people facing the same kind of fear. They all worried about showing anyone who they really were.

"Just tell me, Cam."

The story spilled out of him, and he wouldn't have been able to stop the words if he tried. "I woke up days after the accident, and it was gone."

"What, Cam? What was gone?"

He closed his eyes. "Half of my leg."

A tiny gasp escaped her lips. She reached for him, but he stepped back.

"Can I…" She paused. "Can I see it?"

He'd expected the question, but he hadn't been prepared for it. The air rushed from his lungs. Breathe, he told himself. Keep breathing.

His lungs finally expanded again, and he nodded. This was his first step to telling everyone else. Peyton. Nari. Even Avery and Julian.

They would all see what that night took from him.

He bent and pulled up the pant leg covering his artificial leg. Cara's eyes slid over the metal surface, taking in every inch.

"You're just like me," she finally said, shooting him a grin. "A robot."

He let the leg of his pants fall just as a loud gasp sounded behind him. He felt her presence before he turned. As the dread built in his gut, pain rocketed up his leg. He grit his teeth, trying to ignore it as he met Peyton's wide eyes.

The look he saw there was one he'd never forget.

# Chapter Eleven

## PEYTON

~ *Peyton,*
*The accident... It broke me.*
*It took something from me,*
*but I'm not going to bring you into my pain.*
*Cam* ~

Peyton turned the volume up on her "get your butt moving" playlist. Jogging at a pace that barely qualified as running, she pushed herself for one more lap around the track.

"Past Peyton is an idiot." She panted, trying to resist the urge to rip her Spanx off right there in the middle of the field. *Who wears Spanx under workout clothes?*

It sounded like a good idea at the time. Normally, before her workouts, Peyton threw on whatever wasn't dirty and headed out the door with a water bottle and a protein bar, but not today. Past Peyton had decided she needed to look her best.

Current Peyton rolled her eyes at herself. She'd been determined to come here and run into Cameron and let things fall into place. And she'd wanted to look as much like the Peyton Cameron remembered. With a brand-new pair of slimming black leggings over her Spanx, she'd donned a cute purple tank top with a soft gray off-the-shoulder sweater over it. She even took the time to braid her hair and put on eyeshadow and mascara—to work out. Peyton was *not* one of those girls who could work up a sweat and still look gorgeous.

She wasn't at the size she wanted to be for this, but it was time. She had to talk to Cameron and try to salvage their friendship. She couldn't—wouldn't—expect more than that. That was a recipe for a broken heart.

*Fat girls don't get the hot jock.*

If anyone said that on her app, she would tell them they were wrong. Things looked a lot different on this side of the situation though. She had to remember that harsh reality when responding to No BS comments.

But after all her careful preparation, he wasn't even there when she'd arrived. Cameron Tucker had never met a Saturday morning that didn't start with a few hours at the track. He should have been there.

*What was I thinking?* Rather than going home, she'd gone for a run, regretting her wardrobe choices almost instantly. As she made the last turn on her final lap, mascara running down her face and her hair flying free of her braid, she spotted him on the bleachers with sweet little Cara. With a pang, she remembered how he called her Care Bear, how adorable they were together. Cameron always made the little girl feel special, like he couldn't even see her wheelchair.

Peyton slowed to a walk, watching the way he was with the eleven-year-old.

"There it is," she whispered. The smile she missed so much. She hadn't seen it in ages. Cameron wasn't always liberal with his smiles, but Cara could usually pull them out of him.

She couldn't go over there now. Not looking like a hot mess. She took a step toward her car, her shoulders slumping in defeat.

"Why do I care so much about the way I look?" She'd never worried about those things before. Before the kiss under the mistletoe.

*It's been eighteen months. We're not the same people we were that night.* But Peyton was ready to figure out who they were now. This wasn't about romance or trying to get back what they'd almost had. This was about a friendship she'd always counted on. A friendship that had nothing to do with appearances.

Peyton watched as Cam wheeled Cara around to the side of the bleachers. She wasn't letting him leave again. It was now or never. If she wanted her best friend back, she had to make the first move. She knew Cameron Tucker better than he knew himself, and he would always be too dang slow to deal with his emotions. And that was okay. She was ready to do this for them.

Fussing with the hair escaping her braid, she took a deep breath. Cameron stood, talking with Cara, his face now far too serious for a chat with a kid. Where had the smile gone?

Just as she was about to announce her presence, Cam leaned over and lifted his pant leg.

She saw it—the metal where his leg should be. His beautiful, powerful leg. But it wasn't there. Nothing her eyes saw made sense to her mind. The very thing that defined Cameron Tucker's entire existence was gone, and she was the last to figure it out.

Peyton always thought she was the one who'd lost everything that night. That she was the one needing the comfort only her best friend could give and that he'd selfishly abandoned her to go train for the Olympics in *her* hour of need.

She shook her head with a sob. Peyton was the selfish one. If she'd truly been his friend, she would have known that nothing short of *this* would keep Cam away for eighteen months. In her own grief, she'd never stopped to think of his. She knew without a doubt that losing his leg had destroyed him. And it was all her fault.

She was the one who made the boys leave that night.

*How he must hate me...*

Peyton tore her gaze from his prosthetic, her eyes wide with shock. Meeting his gaze and seeing so much pain reflected in their depths, like the coward she'd accused him of being, she turned and ran.

Peyton absently drizzled melted butter and warm maple syrup over her stack of gluten-free wheat berry pancakes. Sitting alone at the kitchen counter, her emotions were on autopilot. For once, she ate without thinking about calories. She ate for the comfort it gave her because, more than anything, Peyton needed something to find comfort in. Her mother was still asleep from another late night at The Main and her stepfather was working the insane Saturday morning shift. Who knew where Julian was. Not that they were talking much these days, anyway.

*Cameron lost his leg.* She couldn't process it. She could not reconcile the Cameron she'd always known with the Cam she saw today.

*Why didn't he tell me?* How did they drift so far from each other that something this huge and life changing had happened to her best friend in the entire world and he didn't feel like he could tell her? She'd always thought he hadn't wanted to see her when he was in the hospital because he'd blamed her for the accident. She blamed herself for the accident even more now. Cameron wasn't going with Cooper and Avery that night, not until she'd asked him to get them out of there.

*"What's going on down there?"* Cameron asked. *The shouts below the treehouse burst the warm happy bubble they were in.*

*"It's Julian again."* Peyton sighed, watching her brothers fighting like mortal enemies in the middle of what was supposed to be a fun Christmas Eve party. *"How can two people who look so much alike hate each other so much?"*

*"Let's go."* Cam offered his hand. *"Avery's already breaking it up. They just need to cool off."*

*Except by the time they climbed down from the old treehouse, Julian and Cooper were still going at it, and Avery wasn't making much headway with either of them, drunk as he was.*

*"Julian, just get lost already,"* Avery slurred. *"You weren't even invited."*

*But Julian didn't listen. He broke free from those trying to hold him back and took another shot at his brother. Peyton grimaced at the sound of Julian's fist cracking against Cooper's jaw.*

*"There's blood!" She cried. "You idiots! Stop this right now." She lunged between her brothers, but Cooper shoved her out of the way, and Avery stumbled to make a grab for Julian again. "Get out of here! All of you." She shoved Avery toward the driveway.*

*Cameron's arms wrapped around her as he pulled her away from the fight. "Be careful," he said.*

*"Get them out of here, Cam? Please? Before Coop kills Julian this time."*

*Cameron nodded, pressing his car keys into her hands. "I'll drive them home in Coop's car. You get Julian. He'll calm down once we leave."*

*Peyton nodded, grateful for his help.*

*"Be safe, Pey." He gave her a brilliant smile before he lunged into the fight, grabbing Cooper around the middle. "Come on, Avery. We're leaving."*

*"What?" Avery gave him a confused look.*

*"More beer, dude. We're going to get more beer."*

*"Right, shotgun," Avery called, following behind them.*

*"Get in the back, Avery." Cam leaned a drunken Cooper against the passenger door, shoving Avery toward the back.*

*"Peyton, give me the keys!" Julian demanded, prying them from her fingers. Peyton looked up to meet Cameron's worried frown just as Julian took off running to the street for Cameron's car.*

*Before Cam had time to react, Cooper lunged into the driver's side and slid behind the wheel. Cameron barely had enough time to jump in the front seat before Coop took off down the driveway into the icy night with Julian hot on his trail.*

That was the last time Peyton saw Cameron whole. A few hours later, Addison's parents came home to give Peyton the bad news about the accident. They didn't know anything, but they took her to the hospital to meet her parents. That was where she found out Cooper was dead and Cameron was missing. Julian had disappeared in Cam's car. There was nothing for them to do but go home in the wee hours of the morning. But Peyton couldn't sleep, not knowing Cameron was out there somewhere, hurt, possibly dead.

They brought him to the hospital early the next morning when rescuers found him along the bank of the river a mile downstream from Defiance Falls. By then, Peyton had pieced together what happened. Cooper was driving too fast and slid on the bridge and into the river. Cameron had fought to get everyone out, but he couldn't get Cooper out of his seat belt. Somehow, he'd gone over the falls with Cooper, but because he wasn't in the car, the current took him down-river. After a night out in the elements, he was in bad shape when they brought him in.

Mr. Tucker had refused to let Peyton see Cameron once he was stable. He'd claimed Cameron didn't want to see her. She'd haunted the hospital waiting rooms for days, waiting for Cameron to ask for her. He never did. In the end, she'd left his Christmas present with Cam's father and went home to prepare for her brother's funeral.

Peyton shoved her half-eaten pancakes aside and poured herself a fresh cup of coffee, adding a splash of fat-free cream. Images of that night ran on a loop through her mind. There was still so much she didn't understand, but she should have known something wasn't right. She should have fought harder to see Cam in the hospital. She couldn't help but think if she'd forced the issue and found out about the extent of his injuries then the last year and a half might have played out much differently for both of them.

The back door creaked open letting in a cool blast of air into the kitchen.

"You're up early," Julian said, closing the door behind him.

"It's almost ten, you're just getting home?" she replied. "What have you been up to all night?"

"None of your business." He took a bite of her pancakes and made a face, turning to rummage through the fridge for something more palatable and less gluten free.

"Don't be like that, Julian." Peyton snapped.

"Like what?" He stood to his full height, facing her with a sneer.

"Like Cooper." She regretted the words as soon as she said them. Her brother's face fell.

"When did you get to be so cruel?" He didn't wait for her to answer. The slamming of his bedroom door was the only reply she was getting this morning.

For a moment, she wanted to cry. Everything was just so *wrong*. The brother she loved was finally home, and they couldn't even figure out how to have a conversation. And Cameron… She couldn't even imagine what he'd been through. From the second she saw his artificial leg, it gutted her. She knew if she let the tears come, she might never stop.

Peyton shoved her chair back with a surge of anger. She needed to rage at something. She'd lost so much time with Cam. It wasn't fair.

Without thinking about it, she grabbed her keys and drove the short distance to Cam's house.

Cam's mother worked most weekends, but Peyton was hoping she'd catch her before she left for whatever workout video or infomercial she was supposed to be filming today.

As she rang the doorbell, Peyton's anger exploded. "I know you're home, Mrs. Tucker!" She shouted, slamming her palm against the polished wooden door. "Open this door, darn it!" Peyton might have been the reason Cam was in the car that night, but it was his lousy parents who sent him away to recover alone.

*Who does that?*

"Peyton, what on earth?" Mrs. Tucker opened the door, wrapping a dressing gown around her fancy workout clothes. "We'll be filming today, it's not a good time, and Cameron isn't home. Why don't you come back later?"

"You threw him away?" Peyton shoved past her best friend's mother into the glamorous foyer of their perfect home. But it wasn't a perfect home, far from it. Behind all the glitz and shiny expensive things, it was just a showpiece. A vapid, empty shell Cameron grew up in.

"How could you do it?" she demanded.

"Do what? What are you talking about?" Mrs. Tucker folded her arms across her chest.

"Do you even know your son? Do you have any idea what the last year and a half has done to him?"

"How dare you come into my—"

But Peyton wouldn't let her finish. "If you knew him at all, you would know how much losing his leg would *destroy* him! And you sent him away? Alone?"

"He wasn't alone, dear. He had an army of physical therapists to whip him back into shape. He's been training at a world-class rehab clinic. There was absolutely nothing Cameron lacked in his recovery."

"What is it with you people?" Peyton ran her hands through her hair, the tears finally coming. "It's always about things with you. You give him shiny playthings, and you think that's enough. He didn't need therapists and strangers taking care of him. He needed *family*. He needed me!"

"We visited." His mother fussed with the belt at her waist, clearly uncomfortable with this conversation. "We didn't think it prudent to tell everyone our business."

"You're trying to hide it like it's some dirty secret." Peyton shook her head in disgust. "My family has always been Cameron's family. My mother loves him like a son. He's spent more time with us than in his own home. Every birthday, every celebration, every…Christmas, he spent it with us, and you took him away from that? How could you be so cold?"

"Cameron needed tough love, Peyton. You don't understand. He was in such a bad place after the accident. We didn't know what to do with him."

"So, you stuck him in a clinic? To let someone else put him back together? That should have been *my* job. You have no idea who your son is and what he needed then or now."

"He's recovering, Peyton. He's doing really well now. We're even talking about the Paralympics."

Peyton laughed through her tears. "You people really know how to crush his spirit. You took something he loved more than anything in this world, and you made him hate it. Nothing he does is ever good enough. And now he probably thinks he's broken. He'll never be your ticket to the Olympics, and you're still shoving him into something he doesn't want."

"Cam loves competing—"

"You need to back off, Mrs. Tucker!" Peyton's voice rose

as she took a step toward the startled woman. "Give him time to learn to love it again. And if Cameron never runs again, never competes, you *will* do whatever it takes to show him you love him, anyway."

"He knows we love him."

"No, Mrs. Tucker," Peyton scoffed. "He doesn't. And leaving him with strangers during the *worst* time of his life was a real great way to show him exactly how little you care."

Tears welled in the woman's eyes, and Peyton felt a stab of guilt. But this woman and her husband had done enough to hurt their son.

"From now on, I will be there for Cameron. I will help him discover who he is without running. And if he *ever* learns to love running again, you will let him find his own way back to competing if and when he decides. Are we clear?"

Peyton was surprised when Mrs. Tucker nodded.

As she turned to go, her anger deflated. How was she going to be there for Cameron when they weren't even talking?

# Chapter Twelve

## CAMERON

---

~ Cam,

*You always fight for what you want.*

Peyton ~

---

Why did he always end up back here? It was like the river called to him each time the pain became too real. Each time Cameron was reminded of just who he was now. The rushing waters had taken a lot from him, and yet, it was the only place he could think—the only place he didn't feel like he had to hide.

He leaned against the railing near the bottom of the falls and closed his eyes, picturing Peyton's face in her moment of realization. She'd finally learned the boy she put on such a pedestal wasn't as perfect as she thought.

Cam used to hate how much Peyton idealized him. In her

mind, he could do no wrong. It came from a good place, but it only made him feel the need to hide the slightest imperfections.

But now? This wasn't some feeling of anger he squashed so she wouldn't see that side of him. It wasn't a simple dislike of his rise to running fame.

He couldn't keep this truth from her. Not anymore.

He hung his head, letting the sound of the crashing falls wash away his self-pity. Only, it didn't work this time.

He'd never expected Peyton to be the one to make him feel more broken than he already had.

He pulled his phone from his pocket and pressed his thumb over the No BS icon. He'd downloaded the app before driving away from the school. Knowing so many people at their school were struggling should have helped him feel less like an outsider, but it didn't.

They bravely told their stories. Sure, they were hidden behind screen names, but their words still had an impact.

Cam only shared his problems with a dead guy and a kid.

He didn't know how long he'd been scrolling through messages when he finally turned and found his mother standing a few paces behind him.

With a sigh, Cam lifted his eyes to hers. She wore one of her expensive workout outfits and looked so out of place in the park along the river it would have been comical if he was in any mood to laugh. Joggers weren't a rare thing, but his mother wasn't the typical jogger. She didn't strap on fifty-dollar running shoes and discount spandex. Every workout of hers was calculated to further her career.

Cam was the first to speak. "I thought you were filming a new video today."

She waved her hand as if to say that didn't matter. Cam

crossed his arms, not trusting her reason for coming. To her, the only things that mattered were work and appearances.

"Cam." Her voice wobbled on his name.

He hadn't noticed before, but dark mascara smudged under red eyes. Had his mother, the ice queen herself, been crying?

"Mom, what happened?" He stepped toward her, alarm ringing in his mind. "Is it Dad? Is he okay?"

She ran a hand through her perfect curls. The makeup. The hair. She'd already been prepared for the camera. Why was she there?

"Cameron, do you truly hate competing?"

Cam froze. What was she talking about? "I'm not sure what you mean."

"All these years, we've pushed you, but I thought we were only helping you get to where you wanted to go. Did you ever want to be an Olympic runner?"

"I need to sit down." Cam walked to a nearby bench, buying himself time to think. He rested his arms on his knees as she moved to sit beside him. "How did you find me here?"

"I checked the track first, but you've been coming to this river a lot since returning home."

She'd noticed? For years, he'd lived his life as if his parents neither noticed nor cared where he was.

"Can you please answer my question?" She straightened her spine to prevent herself from slouching. The vulnerability in her eyes might be new, but she was still the same person she'd always been.

Cam sighed. "I don't know."

"You don't know?"

He'd never had to explain this before, not even to Peyton. It was his best kept secret. "I've been running and competing for so much of my life that I never stopped to consider if I enjoyed it. The races, at least. I did love the running. But it was just my life, something I always did. Sure, I dreamed of the Olympics, but I don't know if it was a true dream or one that just seemed like the logical choice."

She was quiet for a long moment. "And now?"

Cam reached down and lifted his pant leg enough to feel the cold metal underneath. "Now, I don't know what's logical anymore."

She pursed her lips. "Logical." She shook her head. "Maybe it's time we all stop thinking about what's logical and start figuring out what's you."

"Who are you and what have you done with my mother?"

He'd meant it as a joke, but sadness entered her eyes and she shifted them away. "Your father and I..." She sighed. "We've made a lot of mistakes. Do you know what saddens me the most?"

He shook his head.

"I'm not sure you even know how much we love you."

Cam focused on the tumbling falls and shrugged.

His mother put a hand on his arm. "We've only ever wanted what is best for you, son. When your father had his Olympic dream taken away, it nearly killed him. He never wanted you to feel like that."

"It wasn't taken away, Mom. He gave it up when he took the drugs. All I've ever been to him is his ticket back to the show, his chance at redemption."

She squeezed his arm. "I'm sorry we've made you feel like that, honey. And I'm sorry it took your friend to make me see it. She has quite the sharp tongue, that one. I'm glad you've had her looking out for you."

"My friend?"

"Yes, the chubby one. Peyton."

Cam ripped his arm away from his mom. "What is wrong with you, Mom?" He stood. "You're just like the rest of the world. You only see what's on the outside. You fail to look close enough to notice Peyton has a bigger heart than you could even dream of." Even as he said the words, he pictured her shock when she saw his leg.

There had to be an explanation for her reaction. "She's the best person I know. She cares about people. Do you know how many emails I received from you and Dad while I was gone? Two. Do you know how many Peyton sent? Three hundred sixty-five. She emailed every day for a year until finally stopping because I didn't respond. She deserved better than your words, and she deserved better than me."

He turned to walk away. "And for the record, Peyton isn't chubby. She's beautiful even if she doesn't fit the image of perfection in your superficial world."

He spared one last glance at his mother only to find her smiling. "Son, I have now been yelled at by both you and Peyton in a single day defending the other. For two people who aren't speaking, you sure do care."

"Of course, I care. Even when I was avoiding her messages, wanting no reminders of the crash or this stupid town, I cared."

"Then why am I the only one who knows that?"

Since when did his mother give him advice? He shook his head and turned to walk up the grassy hill to where he'd parked his car.

The day's note from Peyton's box sat on his dashboard. He'd taken it from the "You" envelope.

---

*You always fight for what you want.*

---

When she'd written it, she'd been wrong. He'd always let other people tell him what to fight for. Not anymore.

# Chapter Thirteen

## PEYTON

---

*~ Peyton,*

*I'm a jerk.*

*A jerk who took advantage of your kindness for far too long.*

*I'm sorry, but you need to forget me.*

*Cam ~*

---

Peyton eyed the top shelf of her closet.

"Don't do it, Peyton," she whispered. "Don't go down that rabbit hole again." Last time was so close though. She tugged the jeans from the bottom of the pile of taboo clothes. The ones that were her favorites but no longer fit.

*Maybe this time.* These used to be her favorite jeans. They used to be her baggy comfy, I don't care jeans. Then last year, they became her fat jeans. And now, they were her "I can't wait to be skinny again so I can wear these" jeans. But if she put them on and they didn't fit…if they were tighter than the last time she tried, it would send her spiraling again. She wasn't sure it was worth the risk.

*I lost three more pounds. I can't get mad at myself for that.*

The temptation was too much. Peyton held her breath as she slipped the jeans on. They fit! Peyton sucked in and tugged the zipper up. They were still snug, but as she turned around in the mirror, a triumphant smile lit her face. She was really doing it. All these months of diet and exercise were worth it to get to this moment. She couldn't remember a time when she'd felt so…light. Like with the weight she'd lost an even greater weight had lifted from her shoulders.

Peyton finished dressing for school and headed out the door. For the first time in ages, she felt like things were going to be okay. She'd find a way to make things right with Cameron. And then she'd figure things out with Julian. Somehow they would all heal and move on. They'd never be the same people they were before, but maybe that was okay.

"Did you see the new data I sent you last night?" Katie met Peyton at her locker during their morning break.

"Yes, I can't believe how many users have joined in the last month." Peyton slammed her locker shut. "This thing is taking off in ways I never dreamed. I created it for people like me who desperately need an outlet to talk about these things, but I never expected it would reach so many people dealing with so many issues."

"It's so rewarding to see such honesty and positive

communication. Scholarship or not, you should be proud, Peyton."

"I am. I just really need that scholarship money." Peyton worried constantly about how she would ever pay for the kind of college education she wanted. Schools like MIT and Caltech were far beyond her parent's meager college savings.

"Peyton, if this thing keeps snowballing, you're not going to have to worry about money for college."

"It's a free app, Katie. And it's always going to be free. I don't want to charge users."

"You don't have to." She beamed, pulling a folder from her backpack. "My mom helped me with this."

"What is it?"

"Everything you need to monetize No BS. After you win." She winked.

"Monetize?"

"Affiliate advertising and local sponsors to start. Users will be accustomed to seeing this type of advertising from Facebook and Instagram, and they'll think nothing of it. It won't make you rich, especially not now, but eventually, when No BS takes the next steps to include more schools in our district, and then the state, you'll generate an incredible passive income. And then... the world." She threw her hands up. "Sky's the limit, Peyton."

"I don't understand half of what you just said." Peyton flipped through the folder. "But I'm going to figure it out. Thanks for this, Katie. You're a great friend."

"Anytime, Peyton. I don't have many friends, so it's been wonderful hanging out working on No BS with you."

"You know, we don't need the excuse of work to hang out, Katie. We can hang out anytime."

"Deal. gotta run, see ya!" she called as she headed down the hall to her next class.

Peyton darted back to her locker for a book she'd forgotten. Rushing to make it to her next class before the bell, she dropped the folder Katie had given her. As she bent over to gather the papers, she heard the absolute worst sound in the world. The ripping fabric echoed like a boom, and laughter erupted behind her.

*No. Nope, not possible.* She did not just split out of her skinny jeans in front of the entire school.

"Mooooo!"

Peyton whirled around at the sound. "Did you just *moo* at me?" Her cheeks flamed bright red, but she did not deserve this kind of ridicule. Today was a good day, and she hadn't had many of those in recent months.

"Yearbook pic," Andrew, one of the jockiest jocks, said as he snapped a selfie with her and her ripped pants. Her cute pink panties with hearts on display for everyone's entertainment—not to mention her dimpled butt cheeks.

Humiliated, Peyton whirled around, looking for an escape as half the football team mooed at her. Her eyes swam with tears as she heard a familiar voice in the crowd. A voice that belonged to someone she once counted a friend.

"Come on, guys, you remember Coop's fat sister, Peyton." He laughed. "Maybe just not quite so much of her." His eyes drifted to her pink-clad butt as she tried to tug her shirt down to cover herself.

"Jeez, Peyton, get some bigger jeans," Meghan Lewis said with a look a disgust. "No one wants to see that."

*This is not happening.* Peyton's blood boiled with rage. She was so sick of it. Sick of it all.

"Seriously, Peyton?" Ashley wrinkled her nose. "Why

don't you try some mom jeans with the elastic waist?" She giggled at her own joke.

"Shut up!" Peyton screamed, her voice bouncing off the concrete walls. "Shut your mouth before I shut it for you!" She took a step toward Ashley and Meghan. "What the hell is wrong with you people?" She ran her hand through her hair in frustration. "Yeah, I've struggled with my weight since my brother died. Cooper was the golden boy of this school—he was your friend, but he was my *brother*. Give me a freaking break and *stop* trying to kick me when I'm down." She glared at the crowd staring back at her in silence. "I know I need to lose weight, but do you all have to rub my nose in it every chance you get? I'm sorry I wear my biggest imperfection for the world to see. I don't care anymore." Peyton's heart pounded in her chest as the anger and resentment that had built up all her life spilled out of her.

"But take a good look at yourselves, and think about your imperfections. The ones you're able to hide. The things you wish you could change about yourself."

"Avery the jock." She whirled on him. "Maybe you wish you weren't such a bad drunk. That you had the willpower to say no so you don't end up like your loser dad." She didn't even feel bad when all the color drained from his face. "You're dating the most popular girl in school. Well, bravo. Do you even care that your girlfriend makes these halls a nightmare for the rest of us?" She couldn't even summon the words for his girlfriend, Meghan Lewis. That would have sent her into a rage, and this wasn't about being as mean as them.

"Addison the cheerleader, maybe you can hide all the ways you manage to make yourself look like that. But what if you couldn't? What if the one thing you *know* you are was tattooed on your forehead and that's all anyone ever saw about you?" She wouldn't say it. She wouldn't embarrass her onetime friend by calling her a bulimic in front of the entire school. It was enough that Addie knew what she was talking about.

"Ashley, Ms. Popular herself. How would you feel if the only thing anyone ever saw in you was your worst flaw? The thing everyone whispers behind your back but they're too scared to say to your face? What if you walked down this hallway and everyone yelled *exactly* what they really think of you to your face?" She wouldn't say the S word. No one, not even the meanest mean girl deserved to be called a slut.

She stared at their outraged faces and wanted to disappear. All the mooing and laughter still echoed in her mind. "Now, ask yourselves what the hell gives you the right to do the same thing to me?"

# Chapter Fourteen

## CAMERON

---

~ *Cam,*

*You make me brave.*

*Peyton ~*

---

*Coop's fat sister.*

As Cam walked down the hall, Avery's words had their classmates laughing. Mooing. Were they freaking mooing? Avery had once been one of them. There was a time he'd have protected Cooper's sister from his own football team and every one of their awful classmates.

Those times were gone.

It brought Cam back to the night of the accident when one of the football players called Peyton names, and Cam hadn't defended her. At least not until it was too late. He wouldn't make that mistake again.

CURVY GIRLS CAN RULE

He ran down the hall, pushing through the crowd who'd gathered to watch one of their own try to hide her ripped pants, just glad it wasn't them.

Peyton stood, fire blazing in the depths of her gaze, as she scalded each person before her. Cam showed up mid-rant. As Peyton spoke, the laughter continued.

"I'm sorry I wear my biggest imperfection for the world to see." Her words echoed down the hall until she started naming names. The laughter died away as they realized she wasn't stopping. Peyton Callahan held every bit of power in the palm of her hand. She could have ended it. Everyone had secrets, and Peyton knew them. As they'd ignored her, taunted her, she'd watched them.

Addison sent a panicked look to Avery, and Cam's rage intensified. Where was her panic when her old friend was bullied by her new friends?

Cam barely heard the rest of Peyton's words as his heart thudded in his ears. Peyton had never wanted to be popular, to be one of them. She'd only ever wanted to be free to be herself, and they wouldn't let her.

If there was one thing No BS had taught Cam, it was that they were all hiding something. Picking on Peyton was an outlet for their own insecurities.

"Now, ask yourselves what the hell gives you the right to do the same thing to me?" Peyton's final words snapped Cam back to attention. He waited, knowing she hadn't seen him yet. She didn't know there was an ally at her side, someone who never saw the imperfections she claimed she had. To him, she'd always been perfect.

One of Avery's football buddies broke the silence with a snort. "Take your preaching to people who want to hear it." Snickers surrounded him.

Avery stood stoically by, letting his friends continue to laugh. Cam didn't care what they did, and he knew neither did Peyton. But Avery?

Before Cam processed what he was doing, he stood in front of Avery.

Avery's angry eyes burned into him. His jaw twitched. "Look who has come to Peyton's defense. Cooper's killer."

Cam narrowed his eyes. No matter what the police report said or what witnesses had told the press, Avery would never see the truth of that night. That his beloved best friend almost killed all of them.

Whoever said don't think ill of the dead had never been in a car with a drunk driver.

Cam no longer cared about Avery's fragmented memory of that night or the fact that he'd lost his best friend. Not when Peyton stood pressing herself against the lockers as if hoping she could melt right into them.

He turned his back on Avery and shrugged out of his sweatshirt. Peyton's eyes widened as he approached her. He held out the sweatshirt. When she didn't take it, he cocked his head. "Wrap it around your waist."

Relief visibly relaxed her as she realized what he meant. Her pants.

He didn't dwell on the fact that it was the first kind interaction between them in the six weeks since he'd been home. Not when she looked at him as if he was her savior as if he could still be perfect in her eyes.

She tied the sweatshirt and stepped away from the wall.

The warning bell for class rang over their heads, but the charged atmosphere held everyone in place.

"You think by helping her you can bring back her brother?" Avery stepped closer.

Cam turned to face him, wishing he could see something of the boy he'd known. "Nothing will ever bring Coop back. Not your torment of Peyton or your hatred for me. You lost your friend, we get it. But do you even know what the Callahans have been through?"

Avery leaned down. "You certainly don't. We all stayed behind to pick up the pieces, and you ran."

Cam's fist collided with Avery's face before he even registered what he was doing. Pain shot through his knuckles, but it was nothing compared to Avery tackling him to the ground and slamming his head into the tile floor.

Cam kneed him in the groin and shoved him to the side, but he didn't get up. Instead, he lunged for Avery, taking out every bit of anger he'd had since that night on his old friend. Blood trickled from Avery's split lip, and Cam was sure he looked just as rough.

Yet, neither boy seemed to be able to stop fighting the other.

Cam vaguely registered Peyton screaming at him in the background, but he couldn't make out her words over the rushing in his ears.

All at once, Avery froze with Cam still pinned beneath him.

It wasn't until Peyton's gasp rang out from the crowd that Cam realized why. Avery's hand snaked over his leg, feeling the hard metal underneath. Cam lay unmoving as Avery gripped the bottom of his pant leg and pushed it up, revealing Cam's secret to everyone in the hall.

"You deserve what you got." Avery shoved him again.

"Cam." Peyton's voice trembled on his name.

"Break it up!" The principal sprinted down the hall with two teachers on her heels.

Cam jerked his fake leg up, kicking Avery sideways. Then Peyton was there helping him to his feet.

"You're bleeding," she whispered. She felt for a cut at the back of his head, and her fingers came away red.

A rush of dizziness overtook him, but he gripped Peyton's shoulder and stayed upright.

Avery still kneeled on the ground. His wide eyes hadn't left Cam since finding the leg. All anger had receded as the three of them remained abandoned by their classmates. Classmates who'd never understood what they'd gone through all those months ago. They'd whispered about it and read the reports in the paper, but trauma like that didn't just fade as the news cycle changed. It altered the course of their lives, made them into people they'd never wanted to be.

The principal reached them, scanning over their various cuts and bruises. The two male teachers stood behind her as if they were bodyguards, waiting to be called to action. Cam knew Mrs. Stevens, though. She could handle herself, and she would handle them.

To her credit, no anger flashed across her face. She sighed. "Stand up, Mr. St. Germaine."

Avery did as he was told. He wiped blood from his lip with his thumb.

Mrs. Stevens turned to the two teachers. "You can head to your classes. I can handle these three."

They only nodded and left.

When Mrs. Stevens faced them again, she crossed her arms. "First, are you two boys okay? Are you hurt?"

"I'll live," Cam answered.

Avery only grunted in agreement.

"Ms. Callahan?"

Peyton wound her arm around Cam's waist, and he was

grateful for the support standing. "Not like these two idiots, Mrs. Stevens. So, no, I'm not hurt."

The principal nodded. "Good. Then you're all well enough to march straight to my office. We need to have a chat."

They followed her through the now-empty halls. The secretary looked up with a smile as they passed her.

Mrs. Stevens stopped outside her office door. "You three wait here. I was in the middle of something when they called me for the fight." She disappeared inside.

Peyton helped Cam into one of the wooden chairs outside the door and then sat next to him. Avery took a seat at the opposite end of the row.

Cam touched the back of his head where his hair was sticky with blood.

"The cut isn't too big." Peyton gave him a tentative smile. "It should heal on its own."

Cam only responded with a nod. He'd wanted to fix things with Peyton so bad, but now as she sat beside him, he couldn't think of a single thing to say, so he took her hand in his, smiling when she squeezed his in return.

A few minutes of silence passed.

"Why didn't you tell me?" Her voice was small. "I mean, about the...about the..."

"About missing half my leg?" A harsh laugh burst out of him. "How would that have gone, Pey? Hi, I'm sorry I ditched you for eighteen months, but now, I've returned broken. Want to put me back together? Great pickup line."

Peyton's brow creased. "Broken?" The word was only a whisper on her lips. "Is that how you see yourself?"

"I'm the *disabled* guy now." He shrugged. "It's how the world sees me."

"Cam." She reached for his hand. He tried to pull it away, but her grip tightened. "Look at me." When he didn't, she added a soft "Please."

Finally, he lifted his gaze to hers. "When you saw it... when you saw who I am now, you ran."

She closed her eyes, a single tear escaping. "I made you get into that car. I asked you to get my brother home. Until that moment at the track, I hadn't realized just what I'd done to you. I hadn't known why you hated me so much."

"Pey. I could never hate you. The accident wasn't your fault. When Coop took the keys and jumped into the driver's seat, I didn't have to get in the car with him. That was my choice, I knew he'd been drinking, but I didn't know how much." He wiped the tear from her cheek, and her eyes opened.

"You aren't broken."

He shifted his eyes to his covered leg. "Part of me is missing. I think that's the definition of broken."

Peyton reached down, keeping her eyes locked on his as if asking permission. When he nodded, her fingers wrapped around the metal. Still, she didn't take her eyes from his. "Your body is not who you are, Cameron Tucker."

When Cam didn't respond, she pulled her hand away. "Cara can no longer walk. Have you ever considered her broken?"

Cam reeled back. "Of course not." When he was with Cara, he barely even saw the wheelchair. All he saw were bright smiles and a fiery attitude. She'd never let it define her.

Peyton's expression softened. "Then why do you think that about yourself?" She dropped her free hand to their entwined fingers, covering his completely. "We're always

CURVY GIRLS CAN RULE

harder on ourselves. It's obviously different. I won't deny that. But what's so wrong with being different? You never wanted to be like those jocks, anyway."

Peyton's words went straight through him, entering every part of his mind. *Your body is not who you are.*

All the notes he'd read from her box over the past weeks had only made him want this moment to come sooner. The moment when he no longer hid. The moment Peyton came back to him.

He lifted a hand to her face and brushed a strand of dark hair behind her ear before leaning in and kissing her soft lips. He waited for her to respond, for her to do something, but she'd frozen.

Finally, she pushed him back. "You can't do that."

"Why not?"

She huffed out a breath. "Because, Cam, this isn't two years ago. I haven't spent the last year pining over my best friend. I've spent it mad as hell that he left." She placed her hand against his chest. "I want us back, Cam, but not like that. I can't do that to myself again. The only thing I can offer you right now is friendship."

It was a start. He'd do anything to get her back into his life, even if it meant crushing any kind of non-platonic feeling.

He nodded. "Friends. I can do that."

A smile lit her face as if she glowed from the inside out. She pulled him into a hug.

He rested his chin on her shoulder and inhaled the familiar scent of strawberry shampoo. There was very little he'd forgotten about her.

When he pulled away, he caught Avery watching them

out of the corner of his eye. The hatred he'd bestowed upon them earlier was gone, replaced with...longing?

There'd been a time when their group of friends had been forged together in steel, unbreakable. Cooper, Avery, Nari, Addison, Peyton, Cam, and even Julian. Things had seemed so easy for them, so simple.

Cam wanted that back, but he knew nothing could be the same as it was. They'd all changed. Once fitting together like pieces of the same puzzle, now they'd been damaged, their edges warped by the water of Defiance Falls. And once a puzzle got wet, there was no putting it back together.

# Chapter Fifteen

## PEYTON

---

~ *Peyton,*
   *I don't want to be your friend.*
   *Please stop being mine.*
   *Cam ~*

---

"I know why I got Saturday school," Cameron said. "But remind me again why you deserve to be here?" He walked up to the school entrance with Peyton early Saturday morning.

"Well, right before you swooped in on your white horse to defend my honor and shut Avery up with your fists, I kinda screamed at the entire school and lost my cool."

"I don't know why I thought you needed defending." Cameron's eyes lit up with his smile—a genuine Cam smile she hadn't seen in forever. The sight of it sent her heart skipping. "You can clearly take care of yourself." His hand slipped into hers, the gesture familiar and foreign at the same time.

*Friends, Peyton.* She reminded herself. She didn't want to screw this up by moving too fast. She'd get her heart broken for sure if she let her emotions run away with her now.

"Well, it's always nice to have backup." She bumped her shoulder against his. "This morning's going to suck, but why don't you come over for dinner tonight. Mom and Dad have missed having you around, you know."

"I'd like that." Cameron grinned, but his smile faded as they watched Avery stomp toward the principal's office where Mrs. Stevens herself waited for them. In jeans and a sweatshirt, she looked more like one of her students than the principal of their school.

Avery stood with his arms crossed over his chest, refusing to look at either of his former friends.

"I'd normally leave Saturday school to one of your teachers," Mrs. Stevens began, "but you three idiots are fortunate you've got a principal who not only knows her students but cares about them too. You three used to be friends. I know you've all been through a lot since your sophomore year." Her voice softened. "You've experienced a terrible loss, but I hate to see how that's torn you apart."

"Can we just skip the lecture and get to work so I can get out of here?" Avery interrupted her.

"Watch it, son." Mrs. Stevens crossed her arms over her chest. "It's clear you're mad at the world, Avery St. Germaine, but I am your principal, and you will speak to me with respect."

"Yes, ma'am," he muttered.

"I heard everything that was said in this hall before you boys started acting like heathens. Peyton said a lot of things she shouldn't have. Screamed them, from what I hear. But she had a point. We let simple words have so much power over us when those words are wielded like weapons against us. Those bathrooms are full of the kind of vitriol you kids spew at each other on a daily basis. I'm sick of hearing it, and I'm sick of seeing it scribbled on the bathroom walls." She pointed toward the boys' and girls' bathrooms where the doors were propped open and ready for them. "Peyton and Cameron, grab a scrub brush and get to work scrubbing the walls. Avery, go behind them and wipe down the walls. I don't want to see a single slanderous remark or offensive doodle on my walls after today. What you can't clean, paint over. I want pristine bathrooms before you leave today. And I want you working together." Mrs. Stevens pulled a desk out of the nearest classroom and took a seat. "If you need me, I'll be right here working on budgets."

Cameron grabbed a scrub brush and a bucket and headed for the boys' bathroom.

Rolling his eyes, Avery gathered up paint rollers and brushes and set off for the girl's bathroom.

"Boys' bathroom first, Mr. St. Germaine." Mrs. Stevens pointed after Cameron without looking up.

Peyton was the last to gather her supplies.

"Don't listen to them, Peyton," Mrs. Stevens said. "You are a beautiful, bright young woman with an amazing life ahead of you. The name calling and belittling hurts now, but it will never define you unless you let it."

"I know," Peyton sighed. "But it's not fun. I'm sorry I flipped out in the hall like that. I know you don't like it when kids swear."

"Your principal had to punish you and hold you accountable for your actions, just like the boys, but your friend, Mrs.

Stevens, is so proud of you for standing up for yourself." She smiled. "If there's ever a next time, try not to shout or swear so much." She winked. "A calmly worded comeback can be more effective than a freak-out."

"I promise." Peyton turned toward the boys' bathroom. "It stinks in there." She wrinkled her nose. "Can't I stick to the girls' room instead?"

"You're a smart girl, Peyton Callahan. You've come a long way since Cooper died. You're healing, sweetheart. I need you to help those two." She nodded toward the bathroom. "I Lysoled the crap out of that room before you guys got here." She tossed a pair of rubber gloves at her.

"Thanks, Mrs. Stevens." Peyton followed the boys into the bathroom, clutching her cleaning supplies.

"No one even reads this stuff," Avery muttered as he slathered the cinder block walls with cleaning solution while Cameron moved behind him, scrubbing the worst of the graffiti with a scrub brush.

"You're a popular guy, Avery," Peyton said. "You have friends and girlfriends. Football and good grades—you're who most guys want to be in high school. You might not deign to read this stuff, but there are plenty of people who do." She went to work on a lewd drawing of a cheerleader on her knees in front of the football team. Almost anyone would recognize the cheerleader was meant to be Ashley Richardson. No matter what her sex life was or wasn't, she didn't deserve to be the butt of a joke on the boys' restroom wall. Not when she couldn't even defend herself.

As Peyton scrubbed, the marker faded. She didn't like Ashley, but a feeling of sister solidarity wouldn't let her leave this bathroom until every inch of that drawing was gone.

They worked quietly for a long time, the scrape of bristles

against concrete the only sound. Peyton's mind filled with all the hateful callous things the boys of Twin Rivers High had to say about the girls.

"Don't go in there, Peyton," Avery said as she moved to the handicap stall.

"What? Why?" She went anyway. It took her a moment to comprehend what she was seeing. Four lists. Freshman, Sophomore, Junior, and Senior. The lists ranked the girls of each year, but Peyton focused on the senior list.

### Top Tens of Twin Rivers High: Senior class

1.) The hot/mean girl - Meghan Lewis
2.) The cute girl - Mallory Pierce
3.) Hot nerd - Nari Won Song
4.) The dumb girl - Jenna Jacobs
5.) The ugly girl - Leslie Barns
6.) The fat girl - Peyton Callahan
7.) The weirdo - Katie Whitmore
8.) Best boobs - Peyton Callahan
9.) Best butt - Addison Parker
10.) Best kiss - Ashley Richardson

"I forgot about this." Cameron frowned. "I never gave it much thought before."

"How long has this garbage been here?" Peyton's eyes burned with tears of fury. Not because she saw her own name up there twice, but for every girl on these lists who didn't even know about it.

"It's tradition," Avery said, standing behind her.

"What's wrong with you?" She swatted him with her rubber gloves.

"Hey, I didn't do this." He took a step back. "Don't take it out on me. That's been up there for years. It gets painted over, and someone always puts it back. New classes come in, and it starts all over again."

"You guys are disgusting. For gosh sake, women do not exist for your entertainment. We aren't here for you to ogle and rank like prize livestock at the county fair."

"We didn't do this, Peyton," Avery insisted.

"Then man up and put a stop to this before another class of freshman girls ends up disrespected on this wall."

"She's right," Cameron said. "Half of us sit back and let this happen. We're as bad as the jerks who did this. Now let's clean it up and make sure it stays that way."

"Fine." Avery sighed. "But you really do have nice boobs." He nudged Peyton playfully, chancing a smile at the joke.

Peyton rolled her eyes, reaching into her bucket to grab her brush and slinging the nasty soapy water at him.

"Ooh, Callahan, that's not nice. You're going to pay for that." Avery took a step back to grab his own bucket. "It was a compliment."

Murky water slapped him in the face.

"You too, Tucker? I see how it is." Avery flung water back at Peyton and Cam.

"Oh, that's so gross!" She squealed. "The toilet water's probably cleaner." She flicked her brush at Cameron.

"Hey foul! I'm on your side, Pey." He splattered her with water, and suddenly, the bathroom filled with laughter and dirty water. They were all soaked by the time their buckets were empty.

Avery gave Cameron a friendly shove, but Cam's prosthetic foot slipped in the water, and he went down hard on the ground.

"Hey, man, I'm sorry." Avery's voice wavered as he stared at Cam's leg.

"Whoops!" Peyton laughed, not paying attention to the way Cam's face flushed when he realized his pants leg had shifted to reveal his artificial leg.

She smiled down at him, offering her hand like she would for anyone. He smiled back as he took it. She loved the way his eyes shone when he really smiled. It was so good to see a glimmer of her best friend again.

"Hey, would you look at that?" Peyton pointed at Avery's nearly transparent white shirt. "Avery's got nice boobs too."

Avery smiled, flexing his pecs. "Too bad the one girl I actually like doesn't give a crap about appearances."

Peyton looked to him in confusion. His girlfriend cared about appearances more than anyone she knew. Was Meghan not the girl he was talking about? Maybe Avery wasn't such a lost cause after all. She snapped out of her thoughts, wanting to enjoy the small moment between them.

"She sounds like good people." Peyton laughed. It felt so good to laugh with her old friends again. After all this time... maybe they were healing.

# Chapter Sixteen

## CAMERON

---

*~ Cam*
*No matter what happens,*
*we'll always be there for each other.*
*Peyton ~*

---

Peas were an interesting thing, weren't they? All green and round. Cam stared down at his plate, pushing the tiny green orbs around, trying not to feel the glances from each member of the Callahan family. To say dinner was awkward would be an understatement.

Eating at the Callahan house used to be a normal occurrence for Cam. It happened more often than he sat down with his own family. But the last time he'd eaten with that family, Cooper sat across from him. There'd been laughter, fun never lacking in that house.

Now, the same face stared at him across the table, but it belonged to Julian. He didn't look angry, or even scornful, only confused by Cam's presence.

If he were being honest, Cam was confused too. How had he let this family become strangers?

Cam lifted his gaze to find Mr. Callahan smiling at him as if he couldn't quite believe his eyes. "Would you like some more potatoes, Cam?"

"No." Cam set his fork down. "Thank you."

Mr. Callahan set the bowl back on the table. "Sofia will be so sad she missed you, son. She couldn't get away from the dinner rush at the diner tonight."

Cam offered him a tight smile. "Thank you for having me." He'd already said that twice, but he didn't know what else to say. Surely, the Callahans thought differently of him now. Had Peyton told them about his leg? Julian would have heard the truth at school. It had already spread through the student body. To Julian's credit, he hadn't brought it up. Cooper would have. He'd have given Cam endless ribbing about it, assuming Cam wouldn't mind. But Cooper's jokes had always held a bit of criticism in them. He'd mastered the art of masking disdain with humor.

"Dad." Peyton shook her head. "You've already offered him more food almost a dozen times. Cam doesn't want to waddle out of here."

"I'm sorry, honey." Mr. Callahan rubbed his chin. "I just can't quite believe Cam is sitting here with us. We've missed you around here, boy. Losing one son in the accident was hard enough, but losing Julian for a while, and then a third son too..." He swallowed and closed his eyes. "Ignore me, kids." He opened his eyes, his gaze landing on Cam. "Tonight is a good night. I won't ruin it with thoughts of the past."

Peyton's smile lit the room, and Cam allowed himself a small one as well. He'd known the Callahans thought of him as family, but he'd never considered what his disappearance would do to them. When his own parents kept a cold distance, he'd had Mr. and Mrs. Callahan to turn to.

He cleared his throat. "It's good to be back."

Peyton turned her megawatt smile on him.

Julian lowered his eyes to his plate as if it was some work of art he couldn't look away from. He'd barely said a word the entire meal. For the first time, Cam truly thought about how empty this big house must have been in all the time both he and Julian had been away dealing with their grief.

Peyton and her father looked to each other as if they couldn't believe their luck. Cam once thought leaving was the hardest thing he could ever go through, but maybe it hurt more to be left behind.

His thoughts were cut short by a banging on the front door. It stopped for a moment before beginning again.

Julian slid out of his seat. "I'll see who it is." He left the room, and they heard the door open. Avery's slurred voice filtered in to them.

"I know he's here."

"Avery, have you been drinking?" Julian paused. "Did you drive here?"

Mr. Callahan got up, and Cam and Peyton quickly followed him to the door where Avery swayed on the front step.

"Avery." Mr. Callahan was calm. He knew Avery almost as well as he knew Cam. "Are you all right, son?"

Julian stuck his head out the door, his eyes sweeping the darkened street. "His car isn't here."

"I walked." Avery crossed his arms. "S'not far."

Cam's brow creased. Avery lived a few neighborhoods over, about a mile from Peyton.

Mr. Callahan placed a hand on Avery's arm. "What can we do for you, son?"

Avery stepped back. "I know Cam is here. I saw his car." His angry eyes found Cam standing behind Julian. "We need to talk."

Mr. Callahan stepped in front of Cam. "I don't think that's such a good idea in your state. Come, let me drive you home."

"Not before I know."

"Know what?" Julian shouldered his dad out of the way. "What could you possibly want with Cam? We all know about your fight. I won't let you hit him again."

Julian's words surprised Cam. It was almost as if he was defending him.

"The truth!" Avery demanded. "I want the truth."

Cam studied Avery's swaying frame. His rumpled clothes. His hazy eyes. Everyone deserved the truth even if it meant altering the way you once saw someone you'd idolized.

"I'll talk to him." Cam stepped forward.

"Cam." Worry tinged Peyton's sigh.

He gripped her hand, squeezing once before dropping it. "We'll be fine."

Mr. Callahan gave him an approving nod. "You three can talk on the front porch."

Three? Cam had planned to get Avery alone to hash everything out. He hadn't considered that Julian deserved to be there as much as he did.

Mr. Callahan pulled Peyton back into the house as Cam and Julian stepped by Avery, taking up positions on opposite ends of the porch. As the door shut, Avery stuck his hands in his pockets.

"You're an idiot, Avery." Julian's words hung in the air between them. "What, are you just a drunk meathead now? Teasing people in the halls, fighting those you once considered friends, and getting drunk by dinner time?"

Avery dropped to sit on the steps and buried his face in his hands. "I'm not... This isn't..."

"What? Spit it out."

"Until tonight, I hadn't touched a drop of alcohol since the night..."

He didn't need to finish that sentence. They all knew the night he was referring to. Others tried to understand. Peyton, Nari, and Addison had been at the party. They too dealt with the pain of what happened. But none of them had been in that car. They didn't hear rushing water every time they closed their eyes. Their grief wasn't controlled by nightmares of drowning. They didn't know what it was like to feel as if their life was about to end.

They hadn't seen Cooper in the end, been unable to save him.

Cam's eyes traveled from Julian to Avery. Julian had left town like Cam, but Avery stayed. He fielded the questions and suffered the stares.

He claimed he remembered nothing, but the pain in his eyes as he lifted them showed his lies.

"How much?" Cam asked.

"What?" Avery twisted his body to face Cam.

"How much do you truly remember?"

"Nothing." It was Julian who spoke. "He's been claiming to not remember the accident at all."

"It's a lie." Cam crossed the wooden planks until he stood looking down at Avery. "Isn't it?"

Avery's shoulders hunched forward. "I thought…if I could claim you were driving, if I could make myself believe it, then there was a reason. There was someone to blame." He rubbed the back of his neck, refusing to look up at Cam. "Someone who wasn't Cooper. After a while, I really did start believing it. My memories are hazy, I wasn't lying about that."

Cam grit his teeth. "How much?"

Avery's voice held no emotion. "We were crossing the bridge when we hit ice and went over. I remember that." He closed his eyes. "We hit the water, and the impact sent a jarring force through us. The last thing I can see is water flooding into the car, and I hear Julian's voice, screaming from the bridge, before he jumped into the water after us. I see it every time I close my eyes. But that's it."

Cam lowered himself to sit beside Avery. "I wish I had been driving. Then I'd have someone to blame as well. Then I wouldn't have to try so hard to keep myself from hating Cooper." He sucked in a breath. "You and I got out of the car. I got you to shore but went back to help Julian and Cooper. I didn't make it back to the car before going over the falls."

Julian had been silent through most of the exchange. "I was on the hood of the car, trying to get Coop out. But I was thrown off before hitting the falls. Cooper was still in the car." He rubbed his face. "It's okay to blame him, you know. I do."

Avery shook his head. His words no longer slurred as he sobered quickly. "It's not. One accident can't change every-thing we knew about Coop. He was my best friend, the best man I knew."

No one spoke for a moment before Julian sat beside them. "I wish I knew that version of him. I wish he was the person you thought he was."

Avery scowled. "What are you talking about? You were his brother. You're supposed to miss him as much as I do."

Julian leaned forward with his elbows resting on his knees. Cam studied him. He'd known the brothers well enough to see when there was something one of them wasn't saying. Avery had always hero-worshipped Cooper, failing to see any flaw.

What had Julian seen?

"That's the problem." Julian refused to look at them. "I do miss him, and I don't want to. You say you want the truth of that night. There were other things happening besides the crash. Cooper wasn't the man you thought he was. There was a darkness inside him, and I saw it at the party before he even got behind the wheel. If I told you the truth, Avery, you wouldn't believe me." He climbed to his feet, ready to walk away from them.

Avery jumped up, shoving Julian back. "He's dead! What more do you want from him?"

Julian stepped forward, his face inches from Avery's. "I want him to turn back the clock. I want to erase everything that happened that night. You aren't as ignorant as you seem. You were there at the party. The only reason you didn't see the real Coop that night is because you chose not to see it."

Avery reeled his head back and snapped it forward, slamming it into Julian's. Julian twisted his hands in Avery's shirt, ready to punch him, when Mr. Callahan opened the door. All three boys froze.

"Do you boys really think Cooper would have wanted this for any of you?" He placed a hand on Julian's, forcing him to release Avery. "Julian knew Cooper better than even I did. I don't want to know what happened that night, but I do know it shouldn't put you boys against each other. Whatever his actions were, they were his and his alone."

Julian blew out a breath. "You're right, Dad."

Cam fixed his eyes on Avery. "We all lost a lot."

Avery's gaze drifted to Cam's leg, and all anger drained out of him.

Cam continued. "I thought I was alone. After the accident, I felt like no one would possibly accept me, no one would understand."

When he didn't continue, Mr. Callahan spoke. "You should have helped each other. You were all such good friends. I can't begin to imagine what you all went through, but that night broke this town and this family. It's taken us a long time, but nothing is gone forever. Nothing is unfixable. Even a group of friends who've suffered more than they should ever have to."

Avery shook his head. "We weren't just broken. Part of us is missing. We can't ever come back from that. I'm sorry, Mr. C, but we are different people now." He walked down the steps and paused, his back still to them. "I..." He sighed, hanging his head. Without another word, he left the way he'd come.

Peyton appeared on the porch. "Are you going to come back inside?"

Wordlessly, Cam walked to her, ignoring her father's or brother's presence. He wrapped his arms around her, needing the comfort only she could give.

She returned the hug. "Please, come in."

He shook his head. "I'm sorry. I need to go." But he didn't let go, not yet.

Mr. Callahan and Julian entered the house, leaving the door cracked open.

Peyton's hands rubbed circles on his back, calming his frayed nerves. Every time he had to recount the night of the accident, it all came back to him. And for once, he didn't feel trapped in that car. The bubbling waters didn't rise above his head. For once, he could breathe.

On Monday, life seemed almost back to normal. Cam's classmates avoided him, whispering behind their hands. He'd always been talked about, but now life was split into two eras. BA—Before Accident—and AA—After Accident. Before, they'd discussed him in reverent tones. He was the boy who'd rise above their small town to do great things— namely the Olympics. He'd never been interested in popularity and generally ignored most of the other students.

Now, their gossip had turned from his bright future to his tragic past. Eyes bounced from his face—once beloved by the girls of Twin Rivers—to his leg. He was a curiosity to them. A sideshow.

And he didn't care. Not anymore. All he'd ever needed was Peyton, and now he had her. Maybe not the way he wanted, but he'd take whatever she'd give him, and at that moment, it was her soft smile as he joined her at her locker.

He leaned against the cold metal row as she hid her face behind the swinging door.

"This is good, Pey." He pushed her locker halfway shut so he could look at her. "Like old times."

"Why, whatever do you mean, Cameron Tucker?" She

flashed him another of her heart-melting grins. "This is just a normal day." She leaned closer. "I know nothing of a year and a half where you didn't walk these halls, let alone over a month of you avoiding me in them."

He shook his head with a grin. If she wanted to forget about everything, who was he to argue?

She slid her books into her bag and slammed the locker shut before slipping her arm into his. Peyton had always been a toucher. Whether it was a hug or just a squeeze to the arm, it was how she showed she cared.

And he loved that about her. She may not be more than his friend, but being this close to her still felt right. As they started walking, she looked sideways at him.

When he met her gaze, she shifted her eyes away as if she hadn't meant to be caught staring. He suppressed a smile, realizing she was just as happy as he was to be back together. *As friends*, he reminded himself.

Together, they were able to ignore all the eyes following them. They'd always existed in their own world, a world Cam had once thought gone forever.

Peyton jerked Cam to a stop as a roar of laughter filled the air. A few guys from the football team stood huddled together. Their stares made it evident who they were talking about.

Peyton tensed, and Cam knew she was waiting for the words that cut like a knife.

"Look who it is." Carlson Rogers, star linebacker, began. He bent forward, making a loud "riiiip" sound. His friends laughed, and it was only then Cam saw Avery.

He didn't join in the joke as he met Cam's gaze for just a moment before shoving Carlson back against the lockers. "Cut it out, man."

But Carlson wasn't done. His eyes fixed on Cam, and he grinned. "Figures the fat girl would be the one to take pity on the gimp."

Cam stood stock still as that word bounced around his mind, trying to do as much damage as possible. Gimp. Gimp. Gimp.

He barely registered Avery decking Carlson or his shouted "Don't ever say that again."

Peyton's hand found his. "It's just a word, Cam." Cam's breathing evened as he looked at her. He'd never understood how much words could hurt before, but she had. Peyton had been picked on for years, even when Coop was around to put a stop to it.

Cam had never known how strong she truly was.

"Just a word, Cam," she whispered. "You're the only one who can give their words the power to hurt you."

He released a sigh and stepped toward where Avery had Carlson pinned to the locker. "Let him go, Avery. He isn't worth it."

Avery released his friend, not meeting Cam's eyes.

Julian stepped up beside Peyton, appearing ready to step in if need be. Cam shook his head.

Peyton pulled Cam back. "Let's just go."

Cam waited one beat longer, but Avery and Julian remained silent. Finally, he let Peyton drag him down the hall. He no longer cared about Carlson's words. Avery had defended him. He wasn't delusional enough to think it meant anything more than Avery finding the conscience he'd once had. But it was a start.

Maybe the Avery he'd known back then was still in there somewhere and only needed a reason to come out.

# Chapter Seventeen

## PEYTON

~ *Peyton,*

*I need you. But you'll never know that*
*because I won't send this email.*
*I like to believe that somehow you can feel it.*
*Cam ~*

"You're looking lovely, Peyton," Mrs. Jones said. She and her husband were frequent flyers at The Main during the senior citizen rush. "How much have you lost dear?"

"Oh, last time I checked, about thirty-eight pounds." Peyton smiled as she refilled their iced tea glasses. These days, Peyton wasn't constantly obsessing over her weight loss. She was feeling more and more like her old self, happy to live her life with moderation, healthy foods, and regular exercise no matter what number the scale happened to say. She'd get back to her normal weight soon enough.

"Losing some weight before prom season, eh? Good plan, kiddo," Mr. Jones—never a man with much tact—gave her a wink. "The young men will be lining up at your door in no time."

"Eh, I'm not worried about dates or boys." She smiled. "As long as I have my friends, I'm a happy girl." She glanced over her shoulder to where Cameron and Nari sat at the counter, arguing about video games while they waited for her shift to end.

"Well, young Cameron can't keep his eyes off you," Mrs. Jones said in a hushed voice.

"The Tucker boy? I'm sure he's beating 'em off with a stick, a good-looking athlete like that."

"That's not something we say anymore, Richard. Girls like Peyton have so much more going for them than we did back in my day. Lots of choices that don't involve boys. Isn't that right dear?"

"You know it, Mrs. Jones," Peyton said. "I'm working my butt off for a scholarship to MIT."

"MIT?" Mr. Jones gave an impressed nod. "You keep your mind on the books, young lady."

"Yes, sir." She smiled as she handed him the check. "Have a good night." She finished clearing their table and took the dishes back to Julian in the kitchen.

"Peyton, honey, was that your last table?" her mom asked from her spot behind the grill.

"Yeah, I just need to finish my side tasks and I'm done."

"Go ahead and clock out, I have your dinner ready. Nari and Cam look hungry, and I know they're waiting for you."

Peyton's mother put the finishing touches on the three dishes in front of her.

"Hey, thanks! I'm starving." Peyton punched her timecard and washed her hands.

"I worry you're not eating enough." Her mom frowned. "You've been leaning toward the vegan dishes lately, and that's fine, but I want to make sure you're getting enough protein and a healthy calorie intake. You look fantastic, but you've lost a lot of weight in the last six months. You should think about maintenance over loss soon."

"I'm good, Mom." Peyton squeezed her mother's hand. "I had a hard time finding the balance I've needed in my diet, but I'm in a good place."

"Tofu or chicken?" She asked.

"For what?"

"I'm trying some new healthy recipes, so I'm testing you and your friends. I've got avocado, brown rice, and salmon street tacos for Cam and Tahini-Lemon Quinoa with asparagus for Nari."

"Ohh, that sounds good. Can I have that too?"

"I made you light alfredo with spaghetti squash, mushrooms, zucchini, and I can add crispy tofu if you want to keep it vegan or chicken if you want more protein."

"I'll do chicken tonight."

"Good choice. I also made some cauliflower garlic bread and cinnamon churro bananas with vegan chocolate for all of you."

"That all sounds divine." Peyton took the huge tray from her mother. "We'll let you know how yummy everything is." She flashed her mom a smile, eager to try the new dishes.

"Peyton, honey. It's so good to see that beautiful smile of

yours again. Tell Cam he's on my list if he messes things up again." She winked as Peyton rolled her eyes.

"Your mom is a culinary genius." Cam tossed his napkin aside and stretched.

"That was definitely some of her top-shelf cooking," Peyton agreed.

"I don't even like bananas." Nari shoved her glasses up her nose. "But that churro stuff was amazing."

"I mean, my mom has made a fortune hocking her protein drinks and exercise videos to athletes and health nuts, but Mrs. C could run circles around her with this food. She should package that cauliflower bread stuff."

"She's taken on some vegan catering jobs lately, and I think she really enjoys getting away from all the diner food for a change of pace."

Peyton glimpsed Cameron's phone screen over his shoulder. "Hey, what are you looking at." *Is he using my app!* It gave Peyton a little thrill every time she saw someone using No BS, but to see Cameron smiling at the screen, she couldn't imagine how the No BS community was helping him deal with his loss.

"It's this app I'm obsessed with," he said. "It's called No BS, and it's so motivating. No matter how hard things get, there's always someone out there who understands."

"You've been posting?" Peyton's heart did a little tap dance.

"Yeah and commenting on other posts. It's great. There's a rumor that someone from Twin Rivers developed the app as a safe place for students to talk about the issues they're too afraid to tackle on their own—too afraid to ask for help. I know it's just chatting online with random strangers, but it's done so much to help me deal with my anger at losing my leg. I've talked to people who've experienced all kinds of life-altering things, and they've helped me understand that I need to come to terms with who I am now and it's okay to look at my new life as a blank slate. I can do anything I want now, and it's up to me to decide what that is."

"That's incredible, Cam." Tears pricked her eyes. This was what she'd wanted No BS to be. Even if she didn't win the competition, she was so proud of her accomplishments and even more proud of the online community that grew from her ideas. They were the true winners.

"You should download it."

"I'll check it out." She smiled as a girl approached the counter. "Hey, Julian, you have a customer," Peyton called to her brother behind the register. Normally, she'd help out even after clocking out, but not when the customer was Meghan Lewis, the meanest of the mean girls and the most popular girl at Twin Rivers High. Peyton could never understand why the mean girls were always popular.

"Hey, Meghan," Julian muttered as he stepped up to the counter wiping his hands on his apron. "What can I get for you."

"Wow, you really do look like Coop up close," Meghan said.

"Yeah, identical twins usually do." He heaved a sigh, refusing to meet her gaze.

Peyton felt bad for her brother. People said stuff like that to him all the time, not knowing how it kept the pain of his loss so fresh in his mind. No wonder he'd needed to get away from Twin Rivers.

"What can I get for you?"

"Party tray." She tossed her order receipt at him and turned away. Clearly having Cooper's face wasn't enough to capture her attention for more than a moment.

"Cameron." She eased onto the barstool next to him, her short skirt riding up her thigh. "What are you doing here on a Saturday night when I'm having a party?" She pouted her cherry red lips at him.

"Hanging out with my friends," he said politely.

"Who? Fatton and Nerdi?" she said in a singsong voice. "I know you've lost a lot, Cam." She pressed her hand over his. "You poor thing, not able to walk when you used to run better than anyone."

"Uh, he can walk just fine," Nari said. "He's not paralyzed, he just lost a leg."

"Whatever, that doesn't mean you have to hang out with these losers." She leaned in with a whisper. "The people that matter are still here for you, Cam."

Peyton watched as Cameron's face turned bright red and anger kept him silent. Cam never was very good at the quick comeback.

"Um, thanks," Peyton said. "But you know, we're the ones who have been here for Cam no matter what. Whether he was an Olympic hopeful or not."

"I am already with the people who matter the most to me." Cameron's voice came out strained, like he was trying not to lose his cool. "But where were you with your fake concern when I was in recovery for eighteen months?" He glared at Meghan.

"I uh—" Meghan stuttered as Cameron stood up.

"See, he has two perfectly good legs," Nari quipped. "One's just bionic, and we're cool with that."

Cameron flashed Nari an amused smile. "You think I care about you and your popular friends when I've been through hell and back with mine?" He gestured over his shoulder at them. "Peyton has *always* been there for me. She is always in my corner. Every single day I was gone, she was there for me giving me the encouragement I needed to get through the most difficult time of my life. And Nari has been there to give me the tough love and the kick in the balls I've needed to get my life back. You have no idea how amazing they both are. I count myself lucky to have them as my closest friends."

"It's okay, Cam." Peyton stood beside him. "She doesn't know what it's like to have friends like that." Peyton took his hand. "I feel sorry for her."

"Can't you see she's hopelessly in love with you," Meghan said. "It's pathetic. You're reaching too high, Peyton. You should stay in your lane. The wide lane."

"If she is in love with me, then I'm the luckiest guy in the world. Your perception of beauty is warped. Peyton is gorgeous. Always has been and always will be."

"Whatever." Meghan laughed.

"She's not worth it, Cam," Nari said.

"Absolutely, she's not."

"Your fat jokes are old news, Meghan. Just because I don't have the body of a flat-chested eleven-year-old boy doesn't mean I'm not healthy and beautiful in my own way. I know that now. I lost sight of that for a long time, but I'm figuring out how to be me again.

"Here's your order." Peyton's mom dropped a party tray on the counter. "On the house."

Meghan looked at her in surprise.

"Nari and Peyton are both beautiful, sweet girls. If I ever hear you call my daughter 'Fatton' or her friend 'Nerdi' *ever* again, I'll be having a serious talk with your mother. Mrs. Lewis and I go way back, and I know she would be mortified if she knew her daughter was a bully."

"I-I'm sorry. I-I didn't realize you were there."

"It shouldn't matter if I'm here or not." Peyton's mom fumed. "You know they call you 'The Meg,' right?" She crossed her arms over her chest.

"Uh, everyone calls me Meg," she said, rolling her eyes. "My name's Meghan."

"No darling. Surely, you've heard them call you 'Megalodon' behind your back? I'm just a PTA mom, and even I know that."

Meghan's cheeks flushed pink. "Megadone rhymes with megaphone. I'm a cheerleader, it's cute."

"Oh, honey, no." Peyton's mom shook her head. "Meg-a-lo-don. Google it. The Megalodon is a big giant of a shark. They call you 'The Meg' because you're bloodthirsty and mean, just like a shark. I don't allow bullies in my diner. The Main will always be a safe place for the kids in this town. Now get out and don't come back."

# Chapter Eighteen

## CAMERON

---

~ Cam,

*We'll always be us. Peyton and Cameron.*
*I hope that thought makes you smile.*
*Peyton ~*

---

Cam had a secret.

One that could ruin the newfound friendship with Peyton.

For a year after Cam left, Peyton emailed him. Every day. Three hundred sixty-five emails. He'd felt her fading away with each email, finding less to say as the gap between them widened, as she came to the conclusion he wasn't going to write her back.

Her final email came on the anniversary of Cooper's death, of the accident. It had been filled with more profanity than he'd ever heard come out of her mouth. She was angry. He'd been glad when he saw it. So many of the other emails were emotionless, and the girl he knew felt everything deeply. It made him happy she hadn't lost that. He wanted her to hate him, to move on. He hadn't thought he'd be returning to town until six months later when his parents suddenly decided to stop paying for a training facility for a son who refused to train any longer.

But that wasn't his secret.

He'd responded to every email. It was sending his response that had been impossible. The "send" button had been the mountain he hadn't been able to climb. It had taunted him every day. Not just for the first year he was gone, but every day after that as well.

He scrolled through the draft folder on his email program. There they were. Every email. Some pleaded with Peyton to stop. Others told her he wasn't coming back. And one... Well, that one said everything. He clicked on it. It wasn't the first time he'd read his own words, and he knew it probably wouldn't be the last.

---

*Peyton,*

*It's been a while, yeah? I've wanted to talk to you so many times, but haven't been able to. I've been gone now for 230 days. If this were last year, you'd make fun of me for counting, but we aren't those people anymore.*

*I heard Julian left. That sucks. You don't deserve to lose anyone else. But, Pey, I'm not coming back. You need to forget about me.*

*The accident... Pey, it broke me. It took something from me but I will not bring you into my pain.*

*I want you to stop writing to me. Stop thinking about me.*
*I'm trying to forget. Forget the accident. Forget Twin Rivers.*
*Forget you.*

*You can't be part of my life anymore. It hurts to think of*
*you and I don't want to hurt anymore. I can't be happy when*
*you're in my life. We aren't what we were. We aren't friends.*
*I don't want to be your friend. Please stop being mine.*

---

He hadn't signed it. He hadn't sent it. Instead, his own words sat like an albatross on his computer. How could he have ever wanted to forget her? Peyton was everything. She didn't cause the pain. She made it disappear.

He'd been in such a dark place, and her daily emails only made it worse. He'd continued to respond to each of her emails after that, but none were so dark. In her final email, she told him it was time to stop missing him. He should have been happy. It was what he'd wanted. For her to move on.

His last unsent response was only two words.

---

*I'm sorry.*

---

He had been, but it hadn't changed his decision. If he was done with Twin Rivers, he couldn't allow himself to miss anyone there. He hadn't known where he planned to go. He turned eighteen the summer before returning home and could have found a job somewhere had his mother not shown up in Atlanta telling him it was time to come home.

One of his trainers had called her, or maybe his psychologist. Whoever it was, they'd told his parents he was not going to train for the Paralympics. That he refused. His parents thought they could convince him to change his mind by allowing him to come home.

He looked at the clock on his computer. He'd avoided being home much, but today there was someone he was expecting.

A knock sounded on his door. Would his parents have allowed them to come up to his room?

He didn't bother closing out of his email. He had a few to respond to once he finished the conversation he'd been preparing for. He walked across the room and opened the door, his mouth going dry when he found Meghan Lewis leaning against the doorframe. He'd been expecting someone else.

"Meghan." He backed up. "What are you doing here?" He flicked his eyes to the empty hallway behind her, expecting someone to jump out and tell him it was all just a prank.

Meghan only laughed and pushed him back so she could step into his room and shut the door. Her eyes scanned the room. "Cute."

He crossed his arms over his chest as if it provided some kind of defense. "Again, what are you doing here?"

She turned her gaze on him. "I wanted to see you. Is that a crime, Cameron Tucker?"

She said his name as if it still meant something. Meghan had been one of the girls always trying to catch his attention back when he'd been an Olympic hopeful with two working legs. Since his return, she'd barely acknowledged him. "Ummm." He rubbed the back of his neck nervously.

Meghan was probably the most popular girl in school other than Addison and Ashley. She was a cheerleader, and he wouldn't deny her attractiveness. Most of the guys in the school would kill to have her standing in their bedroom. Yet, Cam backed away, hoping she'd get the hint and leave.

She didn't. Instead, she followed him until they reached the edge of the bed.

Cam swallowed as she stepped way too close. "You...you should leave. Go and find your boyfriend, Avery."

She peered up at him through her long lashes. Blond hair fell in waves down her back, never out of place. "Why would I leave?" She brushed a hand down his arm. "You and I could have a lot of fun together. Avery probably wouldn't even care. Our relationship isn't exactly serious."

Cam tried to turn away, but she followed him, still not allowing him any space to think. He had to get rid of her.

"Cammy." Her voice was breathless as she flattened a palm against his chest. Her other hand snaked down the front of his jeans and into his pocket.

And he couldn't breathe. Not because she was a popular, attractive girl throwing herself at him. No, Cam's current state of freeze was due to the anger he tried to keep from exploding out of him. No matter what kind of person she was, he didn't want to embarrass Meghan. He'd have to extricate himself delicately.

Meghan pulled his phone from his pocket and pressed the home button. He'd turned off his lock code after getting annoyed with it not working.

Meghan held the phone up. "Picture." Before Cam could react, Meghan snapped a photo of them. "Aw, it's so cute. I'm sending it to myself." Her fingers worked over the keyboard so swiftly. When she was finished, she threw it down on the bed and reached for his hand.

He snatched it away. "Meghan, you need to go."

"You don't really want that." Her arms slid around his

waist. He jumped when she squeezed his butt. "I won't tell anyone."

The anger Cam had been trying to repress finally rose to the surface, and he pushed her away. "This isn't going to happen, Meghan. I'm sorry, but like I said, you need to go."

She narrowed her eyes. "Oh, right, I forgot. You only like fat chicks." She crossed her arms. "We all see it. The only person who doesn't believe you like Peyton is that chub herself. She'll never be with you. You've been friend-zoned." She lowered her voice. "Frankly, she's probably a lesbian. Which is cool and all, but also means you've got no shot."

Cam's face reddened. He stormed to the door and ripped it open so fast he was surprised it didn't fly off the hinges. Before he could shove her through it, his mother's voice called up to him.

"Cam, someone is at the door to see you."

He'd almost forgotten what he'd been waiting for. He shook his head. "Meghan, I don't know what game you're playing or if this is some elaborate ploy to get back at Peyton for embarrassing you. But I won't be a part of it. You're nothing but a vapid witch. Nothing you say can hurt Peyton because she is the strongest person I know. You want to know why I'm so in love with her? Because she is everything. Strong. Beautiful. Kind. And you are nothing. I'm going to walk away, because I would rather be just about anywhere else right now. When I get back, if you're still here, I'm going to throw you out the freaking window."

He turned and smiled to himself when he heard her tiny gasp as his words sank in. He might regret them later, but he didn't have time to dwell on the fact that he'd just said he was in love with Peyton. One day, she'd know it too.

But today wasn't about Peyton. He left Meghan in his room, believing she'd take his advice and slink out the way she'd come. He pushed her from his mind and entered the living room where a man in a blue sport jacket stood talking to his mother. A few moments later, the front door slammed as Meghan left.

"Jesse Evans." Cam walked forward, his hand outstretched.

Jesse turned with a grin. "Cameron." He grasped his hand. "It's good to see you, boy. The last time was—"

"After I broke the state record about two years ago."

Jesse nodded. "That was some feat, kid."

Cam nodded. "And some article you wrote about it."

"I only wrote the words you said to me."

Cam raised an eyebrow. "With your own spin."

Jesse chuckled.

Cam's mom had watched the exchange curiously. "I remember Mr. Evans, here. But what I don't understand is why he showed up at our door today. We've turned down every interview request."

A heavy set of footsteps sounded in the hall moments before Cam's father entered the room and froze.

His mother regarded her husband. "I thought we agreed to Cam's request for no press."

Confusion marred his features. "A request I didn't agree with but adhered to nonetheless." He turned hard eyes on Jessie. "Mr. Evans, what are you doing here? Cam is not doing interviews."

Cam couldn't believe his father was protecting him. "Dad." All three adults turned to look at him. "I asked him to come."

"You asked him here?" He shook his head as if to clear it.

"You realize he's a reporter, right? For *Running Life*? That's a thing people read."

Cam's lips curved up. "Did you just make a joke, Dad?" There'd been a time when Cam's relationship with his dad hadn't been so intense. Before he became the coach. As a kid, Cam idolized his father. He wanted to be him. That was why he started running—to make him proud. Somewhere along the way, they'd lost their father-son relationship.

Cam clapped his dad on the shoulder. "It's okay. We won't tell anyone."

His dad stared at him like he was seeing someone he hadn't laid eyes on in a long time. He shrugged. "Your old man can be funny."

"Dad, no one is funny when they have to say they're funny."

"Maybe you're not."

"Ooo." Cam cupped his hands around his lips. "My father just made another joke, ladies and gentlemen."

Jesse laughed, not knowing how rare smiles in that house were.

Cam caught his mom's eye and winked. Her smile widened. Maybe she too was remembering a time their home was filled with jokes. It had been a long time.

The lightness wasn't only within those walls, Cam felt it inside him. Ever since getting Peyton back into his life, the darkness had faded away, and he realized he didn't want anger and past hurts to control him for the rest of his life. For so long, he'd allowed his family to change as they all chased his dream of the Olympics. Take the dream away and they'd had nothing left.

Or at least that's what he'd thought in his time away from Twin Rivers.

If Peyton could forgive him, could trust him again, then why couldn't he do the same with his parents?

Jesse cleared his throat. "Are you ready to begin, Cameron?"

"Begin what?" Cam's dad asked.

Cam met his gaze. "The rest of my life." He turned to Jesse and gestured to where a couch and two chairs sat in the center of the room.

Cam's mom put a hand on his shoulder. "We'll leave you two to talk."

Cam put his hand over hers. "Will you stay?" He glanced to his father. "Both of you?"

His father cleared his throat. "Of course, we will, son."

The four of them sat, a silence hanging between them.

Jesse pulled his phone from his pocket and set it to record their conversation. "Cameron, you said you were finally ready to tell your story. To let the running world know where you've been. I'll let you speak freely without interruptions as was your request."

Cam nodded, swallowing. He reached down to pull up his pant leg. Jessie's eyes widened, but before he could ask questions about the leg, Cam began. "My family had a dream." As he spoke, his other problems seemed to fade away. He forgot about Meghan's antics only minutes ago. The tension that had existed within his family evaporated. It was only him and the rest of the world. Easy, right?

It was. He knew what he wanted to say just as well as he knew how to take his next breath. It came more natural than any interview he'd ever done.

He leaned back into the couch, not meeting anyone's eyes. "When I was at the training facility in Atlanta, I thought the accident took everything from me." He smiled. "I have a good friend, better than I deserve. She let me see that I wasn't broken. That maybe the dream I'd worked so hard for wasn't what I wanted after all." His eyes fell on his father.

Unlike previous conversations about this topic, his father didn't interrupt. He didn't scowl. In fact, it seemed as if every part of him was listening, was finally hearing him.

So, Cam continued. "I don't know what I want. That's the truth. Running gave me so much over the years, and I will always be grateful for it, but I need to figure out life off the track. I'm not who I was before, but I'm still here. Not everyone from that accident can say the same." He leaned forward. "Cooper Callahan was my friend, and he died while I lived. I'll never be able to make sense of that. I didn't lose my leg. I was given my life."

As if the words drained him, his body sagged, exhaustion sinking into him. He hadn't known the words he planned to say before he spoke and, as they rolled back through his head, he felt them in every cell.

Jesse whistled through his teeth. "I have to be honest, Cam. I didn't expect that story when you called. I sort of thought you would use me to announce your return to competition. It's amazing this has all been kept under wraps."

Cam smiled at that. "My parents made every trainer I worked with sign confidentiality agreements." He met his dad's eyes once more. "They wanted me to be ready to reveal the truth on my own terms."

His father might have tried pushing reporters on him, but he'd never let anyone else reveal the truth. Cam hadn't seen it before, but his father wasn't ashamed of his broken son; he was protecting the son he loved. When his father was disqualified from the Olympics for drug use, he'd never been given the chance to tell his own story, his side.

He hadn't wanted the same for his son.

Jesse turned off the recording app on his phone and stood. "You're a remarkable young man, Cameron Tucker. My readers can learn a lot from your story. I'm sorry for everything you've lost."

"Haven't you heard anything I've said?" Cam laughed. "I just went on this elaborate hour-long tale just to say I haven't lost anything."

"But the running? Don't you miss it?"

"I can still run and love it for the sake of the sport. I'm just a bit slower than I used to be. I don't need the competitions."

Jesse grinned. "That's a brilliant way to put it." He walked beside Cam to the front door. "Can I ask you one final question?"

"Shoot."

"Why now? This all happened over a year and a half ago. Why did you call me this week?"

Cam scratched his chin, trying to come up with an answer. The truth was, he didn't know. It had just seemed right. For the first time in so long, he'd truly felt like the boy he used to be. Maybe it was learning he could feel anything other than self-pity. Maybe Peyton's words had broken through to him. *Your body isn't who you are.*

His love for her had never left, but he'd pushed it down so far he'd forgotten it was there. Now it was back.

He turned to Jesse and shrugged as he opened the door. "A girl."

Jesse laughed. "A girl?"

A wry smile spread across Cam's face. "Doesn't it always come down to a girl?"

"She must be pretty special, this girl."

"She is."

Jesse only shook his head with a grin, mumbling "a girl" under his breath as he walked out to his car.

Cam shut the door and passed the living room on his way to the stairs. He stopped when he saw his parents still sitting there. "Mom… Dad…"

"Yes, Cameron?" His mother lifted her face to his.

His father turned in his chair.

"Thanks." He nodded to each of them before climbing the stairs, feeling as though he was finally moving forward. As soon as Jesse wrote the article, the entire running world would know what he went through.

They'd know he was retiring from a running career that hadn't even started, yet once held so much promise.

They'd know he was going to be okay. Eventually.

There was one more thing he had to do. He hadn't been lying when he said he couldn't be Peyton's friend, or at least not just her friend. He didn't want only pieces of her, he wanted it all. Every smile, every kiss. She was the best part of him, and he was a fool to think he could have ever let her go.

# Chapter Nineteen

## PEYTON

*~ Peyton,*
*I'm sorry.*
*Cam ~*

Peyton didn't see them at first. She was so focused on talking to Katie. So excited to share the good news. But then she saw the snide looks and the staring. Everyone in the halls avoided Peyton's gaze, letting their eyes return to the letter in their hands. Pink paper covered the lockers and carpeted the halls in the same nauseating shade.

Peyton looked down at her feet, and she saw it. Her name was everywhere. They were emails. Private emails she'd never received. She leaned down, sifting through the pages. She could feel Cameron's pain leaping from the text.

*Peyton,*

*Give it a rest. Your emails are worthless to me. Just stop. The Cameron you knew died in that car with your brother.*

*Cam*

---

*Peyton,*

*We aren't friends.*

*Move on.*

*Cam*

---

*Peyton,*

*Ignoring you isn't working. Nothing's working. I just want to stop feeling... anything. I need you to stop badgering me with your daily emails.*

*Cam*

---

*Pey,*

*I'm sorry about that night. I'm sorry I kissed you and started whatever this was supposed to be. But you have got to forget about me. I'm not interested. I'm not sure I ever was.*

*Cam*

---

*Peyton,*

*Today was a bad day. Your email made me smile, and I haven't done that in months. It's strange the way a smile feels on my face now. Like my face might crack from the unfamiliarity of it. I know you're trying to be the same friend you've always been. But I need you to let me go. I'm not worth it.*
*Cam*

_____

_____

*Peyton,*
*Just shut up, already. Just shut up and leave me alone!*

_____

_____

*Peyton,*
*I'm a jerk. A jerk who took advantage of your kindness for far too long.*
*I'm sorry, but you need to forget me.*
*Cam*

_____

And on and on they went. Every feeling Cameron experienced. Every angry word he'd spoken. Every knee-jerk reaction to her daily emails lay across the floor where the students who didn't really know either of them could trample the words.

That's how she felt now. Like she'd been trampled. These were his most private thoughts and feelings. He didn't deserve this.

She could hear the laughter behind her.

"So pathetic."

"Poor Cam. Who knew she was such a stalker."

"To think she would harass him at a time like that? She should be ashamed of herself."

"Crazy."

"Psycho."

"Dude needs a restraining order."

Peyton barely acknowledged them. They could think what they wanted.

With tears in her eyes, she sorted through the emails, wondering how many times he'd responded to her and then decided not to send it.

*Every time,* she finally realized.

Peyton stood, letting the emails flutter to the ground. She'd written him every single day for a year. For three hundred sixty-five days, she'd sent her best friend gentle reminders that she was still there for him. Sometimes, she'd vented her own sorrow and anger in her messages, but she'd never failed to remind him that he wasn't alone. And then after a year had passed without a single response, she'd stopped sending them.

*But he responded to my emails.* Peyton shook her head in confusion. Why wouldn't he send them? How could he keep all of that bottled up inside? How could he read her emails and choose not to let her know he shared her feelings? That he was mourning a loss of his own. How could he do that to them?

"Peyton!" She turned at the sound of his voice. "Let me explain." He rushed down the hall toward her.

"Explain?" She shook her head. "I can read, Cameron. I have eyes."

"I don't know how this happened, Pey. I don't know who did this or why, but I will find out. I will make this right." He grabbed her arms, pulling her toward him.

"Make it right?" There was no coming back from this. She shrugged out of his arms.

"What are you looking at?" Cameron barked at the gawking students, sending them rushing off down the hall.

"You could have done something about it," Peyton whispered. He could have put them both out of their misery. A year and a half they didn't speak. A year and a half of heartache. For nothing.

"I swear, I couldn't. I don't know who did this to us."

"To us?" She took a step back. "You did this to us." She turned to walk away but stopped when her phone dinged. Pulling it free of her pocket, she glanced down.

The tears she'd held back so carefully before spilled over her cheeks as she stood frozen with a picture of Cam and Meghan on her screen. They were in his bedroom at the edge of the bed. Meghan looked pleased with herself, but Cam, he looked as if someone had been running their hands through his hair as Peyton had wanted to do so many times.

Twisting back to face him, she shoved her phone at his chest. "Guess we don't have to wonder who did this."

His eyes widened as he took in the evidence that he was just like every other stupid boy at that school. "Peyton, listen to me. This isn't-"

"Anything. It isn't anything, right?" She snatched her phone back and took a step to widen the distance between then. "Just like us. When you didn't speak to me for a year and a half, I should have known. But like the idiotic girl I am, I still hoped one day you'd see me as someone other than an outcast at this school. Sure, I was good enough for secret kisses in hidden treehouses, but what then? I always knew you'd hurt me, Cam. I just cared about you too freaking much to care. It's time I grow up, yeah?"

She wiped her face, ignoring the stares of her classmates. They didn't matter when her heart was breaking into a million tiny pieces. She dropped her voice. "All you had to do was respond one time. Just once." She shook her head and turned without another word.

Cam didn't even try to run after her. He let her go. Now she would do the same.

"Want me to kick his butt?" Julian lay sprawled across Peyton's bed, sorting through a pile of pink papers.

Peyton slammed her bedroom door behind her. "What are you doing here? She tossed her backpack and a stack of folders onto her bed, wishing he would just disappear.

"I'm worried about you, kid. This is some heavy stuff you're dealing with."

"It's private." She yanked the pile of Cam's emails out of his hands. "Does no one have any respect for the private pain of two people who've been through hell?"

"Just two, huh?" Julian picked at the loose threads of her comforter.

"That's not what I meant, Julian. This pain…" She lifted the stack of emails. "This isn't about losing Cooper."

"I know. You two have been through a lot, and you deserve to be happy. But in the end, it all circles back to Coop and his selfish behavior that night. Deep down I loved my brother, but he made it hard. And he ruined a lot of lives when he decided to go to that party."

"What happened to set you two off that night?" Peyton

sank down beside him on the edge of her bed. "Please, just for once, give me the truth."

"I don't have all the answers you want, Peyton. All I can tell you is he deserved to get punched, but he didn't deserve to die. He'd had way too much to drink, and he was so angry. I don't know if you ever realized how unhinged he could get when his anger was out of control."

"That's when he was cruel. He'd hide his anger behind snide remarks and backhanded sarcasm."

"Yeah, and that night he was more angry than I'd ever seen him."

"Why?"

"I don't know, Peyton." He sat up, absently shifting her things to the floor. "When he got behind the wheel, I had this moment—call it a twin thing—but I knew he was going to get hurt. So, I took Cam's keys from you and followed. I was trying to stop him."

"He wouldn't have let you." Peyton sat beside her brother, really feeling his pain for the first time. For months, she was so caught up in her own problems she didn't have room for his. As much as she was hurt by their absence, Peyton was finally seeing how much they'd all needed their own space to deal with their losses.

"When the car went over the bridge, I didn't hesitate, Peyton. I dove right in, but I couldn't get him out of the blasted seatbelt. When the current pulled the car toward the falls, I thought he'd survive it and I could get help, so I went back to shore, and the ambulances were already coming. Avery was good for that much, I guess. I watched them pull his body from the wreckage, Peyton. After seeing my brother…dead, knowing we'd never have the chance to grow out of our differences and be real friends, I had to go. I'm just so sorry I left you behind, sis." His voice was raw with emotion, and his eyes clouded with the pain of his loss.

"I know." Peyton moved to drape her arm around his shoulder. "I know you only did what was best for you. We all had to do that in our own ways."

"I missed you." He nudged her shoulder.

"I missed you too."

"Seriously, do I need to kick his butt for saying all this to you?" He rolled up the stack of emails like a weapon he would use to beat some sense into Cameron Tucker's head. "What is this anyway?"

"While Cam was away, I wrote him every day for a year. I never got a single response until some jerk got their hands on Cam's email and printed them – a jerk named Meghan."

"His responses?"

Peyton's mouth turned down in a frown. "Every single one he never sent." She took the emails from him and tossed them in the trash.

"So, you're mad he didn't have the balls to actually say these awful things to you?"

"I'm mad he didn't have the balls to communicate with me. He just kept all this bottled up inside and left us both hurting and alone when a simple conversation would have started our healing a long time ago."

"He wasn't ready, Peyton. He needed an outlet to say all this. To get it out. You were that outlet, Peyton. His safe place. That means a lot more than some senseless ranting he never let you see. This stuff is about him and the loss he suffered. And your incessant daily reminders probably drove the poor guy bonkers." His smile was the first real one she'd seen on his face in so long, she'd almost forgot what it looked like.

"Let's go get some food. I'm starving." Julian stood up with a stretch. "Mom and Dad are at The Main tonight, so we're on our own for dinner."

"Let me change real quick, and we'll go." Peyton stepped into her bathroom to change into jeans and a fresh t-shirt—her standard after school wardrobe. She was excited to spend some time with her brother like old times. She would always miss Cooper, but at least she still had Julian. Julian might be right about the emails, but why had Meghan been at Cam's house? Why had she been in his room? Peyton didn't have a right to be jealous. They weren't together like that. But she'd thought Cam was better than falling for the girl who'd made her life a living hell.

Besides, wasn't Meghan dating Avery? Peyton wasn't too fond of her old friend anymore, but that didn't mean he deserved for his girlfriend to cheat on him.

She shook herself. It wasn't her problem. She needed to forget about Cam.

"Ready to go?" Peyton grabbed her clutch purse.

"My little sister is the mastermind behind the No BS craze?" Julian crouched in the middle of her room with the entire contents of her upcoming presentation scattered across her floor.

"Stop going through my stuff, Julian." She thumped him over the head with her clutch.

"I'm speechless," he said, flipping through Katie's research for monetizing No BS. "Impressed. Who knew my baby sister was a genius?"

"Not sure how to take that, Julian." She tapped her foot.

"I'm darn proud of you, sis." He stood, still clutching Katie's research. "I could help you with this marketing part. You're not thinking about selling this are you?"

"No way." Peyton snatched the folder from him. "I wouldn't want some investor or corporation messing it up."

"Or robbing you of the serious cash flow potential. Come on, let's go get dinner and talk marketing goals. This research is a great start, but we need a long-term plan too."

"We?" She grinned, following him into the hall. "Who said anything about *we?*

"Hell yeah. I'm your first employee, sis. And I'm cheap too. I work for pizza."

"I can't—"

"Don't say it, kid. You'll break my heart. In this family, we like pizza, and we like cupcakes, and we don't count calories because we're all hot. Get a salad if you must, but you're having one slice."

"All right, I can do that."

"Seriously, Peyton, you're beautiful at any size so please stop it with the vegan, gluten-free, no-calorie, no-taste phase?"

"But Mom makes it taste good."

"Mom does, you don't. Those pancakes you make are terrible."

"It's a mix. And they're not that bad."

"Yeah, they are, I'd rather eat the box they came in. More fiber."

"Oh my gosh, you're ridiculous." She laughed as they headed out to his car. Things might be off the rails with Cam, but she was thrilled to finally reconnect with her brother.

# Chapter Twenty

## CAMERON

---

~ Cam,

*You're a good guy, Cam.*

*I believe it even when you don't.*

*Peyton ~*

---

Cam's own words flooded his mind. Every time he thought he was moving on, getting past the emotions that trapped him in his year away, he ended up right back where he started—feeling sorry for himself. This time, though, it had nothing to do with the leg. That was something, at least.

No, this was just about him. Who he was. He knew how his words sounded to Peyton. It was one of the reasons he hadn't sent them. He'd needed to vent, to pretend like he'd said all the things he was feeling. Because that was the problem, wasn't it? He had felt them. He'd wanted nothing more to do with Peyton. He'd prayed she'd just leave him alone, forget he existed.

The first day no email arrived from her, three hundred sixty-six days after leaving Twin Rivers, he'd thought he'd have been relieved, happy even. It didn't work like that. He'd only felt empty, like he'd lost the one thing grounding him—Peyton's words. As long as she continued emailing him, she'd still cared.

He hadn't known how much he needed to know someone was there until he lost her.

He didn't know why he'd kept them. Maybe a reminder of the guy he wouldn't let himself become again. Maybe just out of some masochistic need to remember the pain, both physical and mental.

He lifted his eyes to the empty track. He'd been standing there since class ended, letting the guilt brew inside him.

What did he expect to find on a track where he no longer belonged? Where did he belong anymore?

With her.

He'd blown that. She hadn't even given him a chance to explain the picture of Meghan in his room, but he wasn't sure he even deserved a chance. He wanted nothing to do with Meghan, but he knew that wasn't what Peyton was really mad about. He'd hurt her. His words cut her deeply.

He set his hand on the wooden box sitting on the bleachers beside him. He'd retrieved it from his car. An October wind sent a chill through him and he glanced up at the ominous clouds overhead. Fitting, he thought.

He opened Peyton's box, needing to feel like some part of her didn't hate him—the part that had written these notes.

*I don't feel that way about you. I never did.*

He'd lied. When he'd kissed her for the first time, it

hadn't been a mistake. That memory haunted him alongside the accident that occurred only an hour after. How could the worst moment of his life follow so quickly after the best?

There were only a few notes left in the box. He'd been opening them frequently, using them to find the boy he'd once been.

He held the final three notes in his hand for a moment of hesitation before opening them. Once he read the words, there would be no more notes to comfort him or make him smile when he so desperately needed it.

But he didn't need the notes. Not when he had Peyton herself. She had to forgive him. They were best friends. She was the only person in his life who pushed him, who made him think everything was going to be okay. He reached down to scratch his leg where it met the prosthetic.

Now or never.

His eyes settled on the first note.

---

*You're a good guy, Cam. I believe it even when you don't.*

---

He released a breath. Good guys didn't say such hurtful things to people like Peyton. He was about to read the next note when footsteps sounded against the concrete. He lifted his eyes to Nari's tiny frame.

She pushed jet-black hair out of her eyes and pinned him with her self-proclaimed "Korean Kill Factor." The look she said could make people fear her. In truth, she was just about the least frightening person he'd ever known. Large framed glasses constantly slipped off her narrow nose, hiding wide, innocent eyes. Besides, she was too nice for her kill look to work.

But she also didn't know when to mind her own business.

"Nari." Cam sighed. "I'm not really in the mood for one of your pep talks."

She climbed over the bleachers until she reached his side and plunked herself down with a huff. "Then it's a good thing I'm not here for that." She snatched the note from his hand before he could protest. "Still reading these? I thought you'd have torn through them already."

He only shrugged in response as her eyes settled on the words.

Nari bumped his shoulder. "She's not wrong, you know. You are a good guy."

"I thought you weren't here for a pep talk."

She set the note back in his hand and tried to twist her face into a mask of serious condemnation. It looked so odd on her Cam laughed.

"Hey," she protested. "I'm trying to be mad at you here."

"Oh, well, in that case, carry on." He suppressed his smile. He didn't deserve to laugh when he knew how Peyton must be feeling. In that moment, he wished Nari had it in her to be truly mad. He wanted someone to yell at him, and that wasn't in her.

"You're kind of a jerk, Cam."

He reeled back in surprise, trying not to laugh again at how funny that phrase sounded coming from her mouth.

She huffed in exasperation. "Fine. You're a butt. Is that more Nari-like? Ugh, you'd think I spit rainbows and ride unicorns for how you guys see me. Stop being a jerk, Cameron Tucker."

"I'm sorry."

"I don't mean to me, numb nuts. You really are impossible, aren't you? When they chopped off your leg, did they mess up and get your brain as well?"

He flinched.

A smile broke out across Nari's face. "Too soon to joke about it?"

He shook his head. "I guess not. It's not the worst thing happening to me right now."

"Nothing is happening *to* you. You did this. I'm not going to say you didn't. I know you didn't plan for Peyton to ever see what you wrote, but the fact stands. You wrote really mean words whether you sent them or not. And then you kept them? Ever heard of the delete button? Lordy, I'm surrounded by idiot men in my life."

"Plural?"

She sighed. "Avery was suspended from the team for a week for that fight the two of you thought was such a grand idea."

That surprised Cam. Avery was the star of the football team. "How do you know that?" He hadn't heard it around school, but his drama with Peyton was still all anyone was talking about.

"His mom told mine." She leaned forward against her knees. Nari had the misfortune of living next door to Avery. When their group of friends was still speaking, it worked because they could all hang out in their connected backyard. But now? Cam hadn't been over there, but he imagined it was tense.

"Stop distracting me." Nari turned to face him. "It's been five days since you last spoke to Peyton."

"How do you know that?"

Her only answer was a stare with one eyebrow raised. Right, it was Nari. She seemed to know everything.

He scratched his jaw. "What am I supposed to say to her?"

"Anything. Everything. Stop being so clueless. You're better than that. I know the whole Meghan thing isn't what it seems, and if Peyton really thinks about it, she does too. But that's not the only thing you have to answer for." She tapped the side of his head. "Use this brain of yours. Once upon a time, you knew exactly what Peyton needed. Always. That can't be gone."

He met her gaze. "Can I ask you a question?"

She nodded.

"Why do you care so much? Since the accident, we've all barely spoken. Even you and Pey aren't as close as you were."

She hugged her arms across her knees and looked away. Her hair fell to hide her face, but her words were clear. "I want us back, Cam. All of us. The past year and a half…" She sighed. "It's been hard. So freaking hard knowing we don't have each other. But not only you and Pey. Avery. Julian. Heck, even Addison. It never used to matter who we were, the labels. No one cared that we came from different social circles. And now…that seems to be all that matters."

He was quiet for a moment, letting her words sink in. "Our differences make us who we are."

She nodded, her voice lowering. "But they didn't use to."

"I want her, Nari, more than I've ever wanted anything. Not just as a friend. She's everything."

She smiled. "I have watched you love her for a long time, probably before you even knew what love was. But, Cam, you can't just tell her. Peyton has always struggled to believe she was good enough. It's crap, because she's better than those losers who make fun of her. You have to make her believe in you enough to believe in herself."

Nari was right. Cam couldn't just tell Peyton how he felt. Not after the damage he'd done. She was once again the talk of the school.

He needed help.

Sending a text to a number he hadn't used since the accident, he waited. It was Saturday, and he'd spent the entire night before trying to figure out how to show Peyton he was serious, that he hadn't meant the things he'd written.

The only thing he'd figured out while lying in his bed was how the emails had gotten out. Meghan. She'd wanted to get to Peyton, and she'd succeeded.

Cam didn't have the energy to try to expose her. It wasn't worth it when Peyton was hurting. She was all that mattered.

He'd printed out every unsent email, the ones that had been shown at school and the ones that hadn't. He didn't know when he'd decided to show them all to Peyton, but he couldn't keep them from her any longer. He just needed a plan as to how.

The response to his text came a few minutes later.

**Meet me at the diner.**

The diner? He wasn't ready to see Peyton yet, but he found himself in his car a few minutes later and heading that way, anyway.

He slung his backpack over his shoulder and stepped out

of his car. Mrs. Callahan was at the counter when he entered. She offered him a warm smile. "Cameron." She stepped around the counter to wrap him in a hug. He'd once thought she loved him more than his own mother, but his mother was trying, so he made himself stop thinking like that.

"Hi, Mrs. C." He stepped back, his eyes scanning the diner.

Mrs. Callahan's eyes softened. "She's not here today."

He could lie and say that wasn't who he'd been searching for, but she knew him better than that. He may not have come to see Peyton, but he still found himself hoping she was there. "I thought she worked Saturdays." At least she used to.

Mrs. Callahan turned back to the counter to continue wiping it. "Peyton is at her award ceremony today."

"Award ceremony?"

Mrs. Callahan faced him once again, a question in her eyes. "She didn't tell you?" She shook her head. "That girl... Something tells me she didn't tell anyone what she created. I don't understand her sometimes." She wiped her hands on her apron. "Julian!"

Julian appeared through the kitchen door. "I didn't think you'd be here so quickly." He studied Cam, his lips pursed. When Cam decided to text Peyton's brother, he'd had to force himself to hit send.

"Jules." Mrs. Callahan waved him forward. Julian had always hated her nickname for him, but he indulged her. "Get your phone. Show Cam here that app of Peyton's." Pride bloomed on her face. "She worked on it all summer and entered it in a state technology contest. She could win a college scholarship. All the finalists get to demonstrate their apps in front of professors and tech experts from various companies before a winner is announced." Her face fell. "I wish we could be there." She sighed. "My cook called in sick, and Peyton's father is due back in town today after visiting his sister. His flight was delayed, but Julian is going. He was just about to leave. And no matter if she wins or not, we're having a surprise bonfire party for her tonight."

Julian handed Cam the phone. Cam's eyes widened when he realized he knew the app that appeared on the screen. He'd been on No BS many times as had many of their class-mates from the looks of it. The amount of posts surprised him every time he opened it.

He scrolled down. "Peyton made this?"

Mrs. Callahan placed a hand on his shoulder. "She had help, but the idea was hers."

Nari had been wrong. Peyton didn't need Cam, she didn't need him to make her believe in herself. She just didn't know it. No BS helped him come to terms with his injury, his limi-tations. It made him see that everyone had something broken inside of them. He wasn't alone.

Had Peyton created this to give herself that feeling? To have people who understood?

No, that wasn't Pey. She'd made it to show others, people like him, that they mattered. She hadn't done it for herself.

He handed Julian back the phone. "What time does the award ceremony start?"

Mrs. Callahan looked at her watch. "In about two hours."

"Where is it?"

"The state technology center."

He nodded. That was a two-and-a-half-hour drive. He didn't have enough time.

"We'd better go if we're going to make it." Julian's low voice snapped him out of his panic.

He met his eyes, the only physical part of him that differentiated him from his dead twin.

Cam nodded, all words suddenly failing him. Mrs. Callahan smiled wide and gripped Cam's arm. "Peyton is special."

He sucked in a breath. "I know. I've always known."

She nodded in approval and released him.

Cam followed Julian out the door and down the street to where he'd parked along the curb. Twin Rivers disappeared behind them as they drove away. Two and a half hours. He'd be late for the ceremony. He only hoped he wasn't too late for everything else.

"What are you going to say to her when we get there?" It wasn't like Julian to be nosy or curious, but he'd always been protective of his sister.

Cam relaxed back against the seat. "I don't know."

Julian raised a brow and focused on the highway before them. "Better figure it out."

Cam tapped his fingers against his leg as the silence stretched between them. Half an hour passed, then an hour. The landscape changed, but he didn't notice any of it as an idea came to his mind.

He slid his phone out of his bag and pressed his finger against the No BS app. It opened, revealing all the newest posts. The ones with the most views and likes stayed at the top. Posters could choose whether or not to turn on the commenting feature. Most didn't.

He started his post.

---

*Hello. My name is Cameron Tucker, and I'm a fool. You see, there's a girl. It always comes down to a girl, doesn't it? This girl has been my best friend since before I was old enough for her smile to make me speechless. She was everything to me.*

*Let me tell you a story about a boy who thought he had everything, a boy who lost a lot, and the girl who never gave up on him.*

*This app is supposed to be anonymous, but for you to truly understand me, I can't hide behind an internet wall. I have to be honest.*

*The car accident that took my friend Coop changed my life. Not because I'm now a robot (That one is for Cara), but because it altered how I see the world. I was angry, really angry, for a long time. You may have read some of my anger when my words were spread around the school this week—thanks to whoever did that by the way. You've made this possible. You've forced me to finally admit the things holding me back.*

*This girl I mentioned, she's the bravest, strongest person I know. She's also smart and kind and so beautiful it makes it hard to breathe. Oh, and one more thing. I love her. I'm in love with her. I have been for a long time. And I was afraid. Afraid she'd never feel the same way. Afraid she wouldn't forgive me for the words I never said to her.*

*But I don't want to be afraid. That's what No BS is about, isn't it? Getting over our fears. Shedding the labels we place on ourselves.*

---

Cam paused for a moment. The last part needed to be just for Pey, not their classmates.

*So, Peyton Callahan, I'm saying you don't scare me. Not anymore. I love you. I'm coming for you. You told me we could only be friends, and if that's truly what you want, I'm still on my way to you.*

**@CameronTucker**

Cam's thumb hovered over the post button that would let the entire school see his words. He'd never been one to let people in, to show them what he thought or how he felt. He'd been content with his few friends and the solitude running brought him.

But the biggest mistake he'd made with Peyton was not letting her in. She deserved to have received those emails. The pleading ones. The ones where he admitted he missed her. Even the mean ones. She could have taken it.

Julian glanced at him out of the corner of his eye. "If you hurt her again, I'll end you."

The Julian Cam knew before didn't have the darkness inside him that Cam saw now, but maybe that was the point. They couldn't go back. It was time to move forward.

Cam tapped post. His stomach clenched, and he leaned his head back against the headrest, closing his eyes.

"If I hurt her again, she'll end me herself."

"You got that right." Julian chuckled, the sound filling the car and making Cam feel almost normal, like the past eighteen months hadn't happened, like maybe they wouldn't be tormented by everything for the rest of their lives.

By the time they pulled into the almost-full parking lot of the state technology center, the sun had begun to set. They parked in the first open spot they could find and sprinted across the lot. A banner hung on the outside wall welcoming all contestants.

As Cam stepped into the entrance, it hit him. This was the biggest day of Peyton's high school career, and he'd almost missed it. The ceremony had already begun by the time they reached the conference room. A stage stood near the front, and a white-haired man stepped up to the podium.

Cam didn't hear anything he said as his eyes searched for Peyton, finding her sitting with the other contestants across the room. He found a spot near the back wall and stood next to Julian, breathing in the excitement.

His eyes snapped to the stage when he heard the two words that set his heart racing.

"Peyton Callahan."

He couldn't lift his hands to clap along with the rest of the audience as he watched her step onto the stage. Her face glowed with excitement as a screen dropped down from the ceiling. The audience laughed at something Peyton said, but he was too focused on her to hear what it was. Blood rushed in his ears as an image appeared on the screen. Peyton's demonstration.

The No BS logo stretched across the top with the top post below it. Cam swallowed the bile threatening to rise in his throat as a room full of strangers focused on what was before them.

It wasn't until he could breathe again that he noticed Peyton had frozen, her eyes locked on his.

# Chapter
## Twenty-One
### PEYTON

---

~ Peyton,

    *This is my final unsent email.*

    *I'm coming home, and I'm not quite sure how to face you.*
*Do you still think about me?*

    *One day, I'll be on the receiving end of one of your smiles*
*again.*

    *I promise.*

    *Cam ~*

---

"Peyton Callahan," Dr. Peterson announced.

Peyton stepped forward, a sheen of sweat covering her face. *What was I thinking entering this thing?* Public speaking was not her forte. She took a deep breath, stepping up to the podium to the polite applause. She glanced at her notecards, but the words jumbled around on the page in her panic. *I'm having a stroke, right here. Get it together Callahan!*

"High school sucks, am I right?" Peyton blurted to the amusement of the crowd. "I mean, we've all heard the grown-ups say 'it gets better.'" She held up her hands in air quotes. "I sure hope it does, but that doesn't really help us in the moment. Sometimes we just need a friend. Maybe someone we wouldn't normally consider a friend. I sure needed that two years ago. One night changed my life forever. My brother died in a terrible accident, and our friends scattered to the winds after. We each needed to deal with our loss in different ways. But I found myself alone and in need of a distraction. Thus, No Body Shame was born." Peyton gestured up at the screen where the home page of her app showed for all to see. And then Katie's frantically waving hands caught her attention behind the stage. She pointed at the screen, and Peyton's heart thundered in her chest as she read Cameron's words—the beautiful words he'd written for her—flashing at her captive audience. And then she saw him. Standing at the back of the room with Julian. The look on his face said sorry-not-sorry.

*Did Cam really just say he loves me? Right in the middle of my presentation. I'm going to kill him!*

"My guy, ladies and gentleman." Peyton beamed a sheepish smile at the audience. "He has the worst timing ever. It's supposed to be anonymous, Cam. Way to defeat the entire purpose of the app while I'm presenting it." She rolled her eyes, desperately trying to get her brain back on her presentation. And there he stood, looking handsome as ever, shrugging his shoulders and smiling at her like she'd hung the moon just for him.

"Well, answer the poor guy. Do you love him?" someone shouted. She was pretty sure it was her brother.

"Of course, I do. I always have. Cameron Tucker has been my best friend since we were five years old, and it's only taken him thirteen years to figure out we belong together." She smiled shyly as the audience laughed.

"But I have to give him a break on the last two years. The accident that took my brother Cooper changed the course of Cameron's life too. Once on the Olympic track, he was a rising star. But the accident took that dream away from him. I think No BS has helped Cam accept his new reality. See, in high school, it's all about the labels. The jock, mean girl, nerd, slut, fat, skinny, weirdo, loner, disabled...and the list goes on. We find ourselves trapped behind these constricting labels, desperately trying to claw our way out so the world can see the real person behind that ridiculous nonsensical label. And that is what No BS is all about. Providing a safe place where labels don't exist. Where the kids of Twin Rivers High can talk about real issues we all deal with every day without fear of rejection or ridicule. Because no matter what we're going through as individuals, we are all dealing with something, and we all deserve a chance to redefine ourselves on our own terms.

"I am proud to say the response to No Body Shame has blown me away. As of last night, over ninety percent of the Twin Rivers student body are No BS users. And of those ninety percent, seventy percent are actively involved in this amazing growing community. We have a strict no cyber bullying policy that removes all negative comments from the discussion threads. And for that, I must thank my good friend Katie Whitmore and her incredible mother, Emily Whitmore, for dedicating their time and mad coding skills to the security system for No BS. Together, we have created a streamlined system for monitoring the community and maintaining the complete anonymity of our users."

Peyton paused, glancing at the screen to see dozens of real-time responses to Cam's post. So much love and a positive sense of community poured out of those comments. "It's like this all the time." She took a deep breath. "No matter how the competition goes, I'd like to thank the board for sponsoring the program. STEM studies are so important for our future, and I'm thankful to be a part of such a dynamic community. This program was like a light in the darkness for me. It saved me at a time when I thought my strength was gone.

"And before I wrap this up, I'd like to thank my partner once again, Katie, can you come join me?" Peyton called to her friend backstage. Katie looked like she'd rather do anything else in the world than come out on that stage, but she deserved this.

As Katie shuffled out from behind the curtain, Peyton took her hand, giving it a gentle squeeze. "A few weeks ago, I filed a petition with the board to make an addendum to my original project proposal. No BS started off as a solo project, but it grew from my original ideas, and I could not have made it what it is today without your help." Peyton lifted a certificate from her folder on the podium.

"This is for you, Katie. It says you have served as my project analyst and research assistant. I wanted you to have the credit you deserve for helping me create No Body Shame."

"Thank you, Peyton. It's been a blast working with you." A flushed smile lit Katie's face. "This will look fantastic on my college applications!"

"Who knows, maybe we'll share a dorm room when we get to MIT." Peyton nudged her playfully.

"Caltech." Katie rolled her eyes.

"We've had this argument before." Peyton smiled at the crowd.

"Can I leave the stage now?" Katie whispered, and Peyton nodded.

"To wrap this up, a big thank you to the board and also to our competitors. Er…may the odds be ever in your favor."

Peyton thought her face might crack from the smile stretching her lips. She was so relieved to have her presentation behind her, yet right now, all she wanted was to find Cam. But he was nowhere to be found.

"Congratulations, Peyton." The crowd of well-wishers swarmed around her backstage. "Your presentation was amazing!"

"Thank you." Peyton's gaze drifted across the sea of faces until she saw the one face she was desperate to find.

He looked so proud she almost laughed, not sure if he was more proud of himself or of her.

"You did such an amazing job!" Katie came up beside her. "I can't believe you called me on stage. I was so nervous I barely registered what was going on. You have no idea how much I appreciate the gesture."

"Gesture, nothing," Peyton said. "That certificate was well deserved and the least I could do. I'm just glad the board let me do it."

"People at school are freaking out about this, Peyton.

Everyone is on No BS right now wishing you luck. Oh, and Cam. How adorable is he? I better let you go talk to him. I'll see you later."

"You're so going to win!" A bubbly brunette with the biggest glasses Peyton had ever seen leaped to shake her hand just as Katie left her. "I'm so inspired by your work."

"Thank you so much." Peyton smiled patiently at the girl when she really wanted to shove her and run. Cameron was waiting for her with the biggest smile and a cheesy bouquet of pink carnations in hand.

"You left to get flowers?" Peyton smiled nervously, not sure where to go from here. She only knew she was happier in this moment than she'd been in a long time.

"I was going to get roses. You deserve roses. Big fluffy pink ones...but the store was fully stocked with the worst flowers ever." He was adorable when he was nervous.

"Well, for future reference..." Peyton took another step toward him, closing the small distance between them. "I generally prefer my flowers in the form of fluffy pink icing."

"Icing?" He smiled, relaxing.

"Right on top of the cupcake." She reached for the carnations. "But these are pretty too."

"You were amazing, Pey." He leaned down and pressed his lips to hers. A sweet kiss but not the kiss they both wanted. As he pulled back, his heated gaze sent her knees wobbling beneath her.

"I hope you don't mind my declaration kinda hijacked your presentation. I had no idea it was going to end up on the screen like that."

"I loved it."

"You recovered like a champ." He reached to brush a loose

curl behind her ear. "For a second there, I thought you were going to murder me where I stood."

"Try not to let it happen again," she teased.

"Listen, there's a lot I want to say. And…" He coughed, his cheeks going red. "A lot I'd like to do, but this is your moment. You are going to win this thing, Pey. And I don't want to distract you, so I'm going to—"

"Cameron Tucker, don't you dare leave." She tugged his hand into hers. "Do you know how much I'm freaking out right now? I could actually win this, Cam. I need my best friend right now. Stay with me?"

"Of course." He draped his arm around her waist, pulling her close in a way best friends Peyton and Cam never had before. "When will we know the results?"

"In about an hour. There's at least one more presentation, and then the judges will deliberate. Right now, they're serving refreshments backstage." Peyton darted a look around the room. "College recruiters will be here, and I heard a crazy rumor there are reps from Google and Apple here too."

"Then let's go mingle." Cam pulled her toward the crowd. "I believe you have some adoring fans who want to talk to you." He gestured at a group of girls waiting nearby. "I'm right here with you, Pey, but this is your moment."

Peyton squeezed his hand as they approached the fringes of the crowd forming backstage.

"Peyton!" One of the girls stepped forward with a shy smile. "We love your app." She looked back at her friends. "And we were wondering if you have plans to make it available to other schools?"

"That is definitely a priority," Peyton said. "But it might be a while before we get there."

"We're big fans. It's so great to see girls creating a real presence in the STEM studies world. My friends started a Girls Who Code group at our school, but we're just sophomores. I hope by the time we're seniors we'll be as awesome as you."

"You guys are amazing, working together as a group. Keep up the good work, and I'm sure we'll see you all here in a few years."

"Great meeting you!" The girls scrambled away giggling at Cam as they passed by.

"That was so cool." Peyton grinned. "I have fans. Who knew?"

"Looks like you have a lot more waiting to get your attention." He held her hand as they walked farther into the crowd.

"They're all looking at me." Peyton suddenly wanted to be anywhere but in this room.

"You've got this, Pey. I'm right behind you." Cam gave her a little shove.

"Ms. Callahan, Mike Reynolds." A tall man in a suit reached to shake her hand. "Impressive presentation today. I'm here from Georgia Tech." He pressed his card into her hand. "Have your parents call me, we'd love to show you around campus and talk about that scholarship you're going to win."

"Thanks." Peyton pocketed the card as the next college rep swooped in behind Mr. Reynolds. Pretty soon, well-wishers surrounded her and Cam, and Peyton had a fistful of business cards.

"This is unbelievable." Peyton floated on cloud nine as they continued to walk through the crowd.

"Ms. Callahan." Peyton turned to find a familiar face.

"Mrs. Stevens!" Peyton flung her arms around her principal. "I'm so glad you made it."

"I wouldn't miss this for anything. Here, I want you to meet Mrs. Milburn, she's from the state board of education."

"Hi," Peyton said shyly, shaking the woman's hand.

"Lovely to meet you, Peyton. And your boyfriend too. Cam, right?" She smiled.

"Yes, ma'am." Peyton's breath stuck in her throat. That was the first time anyone called Cam her boyfriend.

*That's right, Cam's my boyfriend!*

"The state board of education would like to talk to you and your parents about getting No Body Shame into every high school and junior high school in the state."

"Wow," Peyton stuttered. "That's amazing, but you should know I don't want to sell the platform. I want to keep creative control."

"And we want that too. No BS needs a young perspective. We believe kids will respond to your app knowing one of their own created it and continues to run it. We can talk specifics when your parents are present, but we have been looking for a platform like this for a long time. Your partner, Katie, will be invaluable for such a big project, so keep her close."

"I certainly will. That all sounds wonderful. I'll have my parents call you this week." Peyton took Mrs. Milburn's card and placed it at the top of the pile. She had cards from Google and Apple too, but she wasn't sure she wanted to go in that direction.

"You're dying, aren't you?" Cam laughed at the look on her face. "I can see it in your eyes, you want to dance around this room and sing at the top of your lungs right now."

"You know me so well. Can you believe this?" Peyton

clutched his hand, so grateful he'd never left her side for one second through the madness of the last hour.

"Time to go find out you won."

"Are you crazy! Don't jinx it."

"I think they're ready for you to get back on stage. I'll go find a place to sit."

Peyton grabbed his hand. "I'm scared, Cam. What if I don't win?

"There's no way you didn't win, Pey. You hit that out of the park."

"Yeah, I did, didn't I." She threw her arms around him. "I love you, Cameron Tucker."

"You're amazing, you know that, right? Like, mind-blowingly amazing. You're beautiful, smart as hell, and you have the kindest heart of anyone I know. And you're going to win this. But even if you don't, you're still amazing, and the platform you built with these two hands saved me. Now go get that big trophy." He gave her a nudge toward the stage.

Peyton couldn't wipe the smile off her face as she stood with the other finalists on stage. Cameron and Julian grinned back at her from their seats in the audience. To see them getting along brought tears to her eyes. She found herself thinking about Cooper. He wasn't always the best brother, but if he were here right now, he'd be cheering louder than anyone.

*I miss you, Cooper Callahan. But I've got to let you go now. I'll always love you.*

Her heart stalled in her chest as Dr. Peterson stood behind the podium to announce the results.

"This year, the national STEM Studies Scholarship Program yielded the largest participation rate ever. It's exciting to see a near fifty percent increase in female participants. I know that makes our male participants happy. Most of us STEM guys are all thumbs and stutters around the fairer sex, so the arrival of our smart and geeky counterparts are about a hundred years overdue." The audience laughed at his banter.

"But on to the awards."

Peyton couldn't hear over the loud pulse pounding in her ears, and she was sure she was going to be sick right here on the stage.

"Peyton Callahan with her incredible social networking platform, No Body Shame!"

Thunderous applause roared, and someone nudged her toward the podium.

"It's an honor to present this award to you, young lady." Dr. Peterson handed her an elaborate first place plaque.

*First place! I won!* She turned bewildered eyes toward the audience, looking for her people. Julian, Katie, and Cameron were standing on their chairs whooping and clapping for her.

"Peyton will receive a full scholarship to the STEM program of her choice, and I'm sure she won't lack for options. Congratulations, dear. I'd also like to ask Ms. Katie Whitmore to come up on stage please."

Peyton watched Katie's face turn green with nerves. She hated to be the center of attention.

"You've got this," Peyton mouthed to her, giving her a nod.

As Katie came up the steps to join Peyton, she stumbled and fell flat on her face. Dr. Peterson leaped to help her up and guided her, red-faced, to stand beside Peyton. "Not to worry, Katie. Not a one of us science and math geeks haven't face-planted a time or two."

"It's okay, don't worry about it," Peyton whispered, wanting to give Dr. Peterson a good long lecture about the labels he was so fond of. Instead, she wrapped her arm around Katie's slim shoulders. Poor Katie trembled like a leaf but managed to give Dr. Peterson a smile.

"Now then, Katie, the board has reviewed the work that has gone into the making of No BS, and while Peyton has spearheaded the project, making it her own, she is right, she could not have done it half so well without you. So, we would like to present you with a twenty-five-thousand-dollar scholarship as well."

"Shut up!" Katie gasped, taking the envelope he'd offered her. "I mean, thank you. Thank you so much!"

"Congrats, Katie, you deserve it, now let's get off this stage," Peyton said, guiding her friend to the safety of backstage.

"I told Katie's mom we'd take you home. Ready to go?" Cameron asked with a smug smile.

"Why? What are you up to?" Peyton narrowed her eyes at him.

"I can't get anything past you." He shook his head. "I picked this up at the flower shop. It's a bit early in the season, but it's brought us luck before. He held a sprig of mistletoe over her head. It was a good memory from that night. Before the accident tore them apart. Addison had hung mistletoe everywhere, just for Cam and Peyton, determined they would finally get together at her Christmas Eve party.

"Congrats, Pey."

"And here we are again." She smiled up at him. After all this time, they'd come full circle, and now it was time to move forward.

"Here we are." Cameron pulled her closer, settling his hand on her hip as Julian honked for them to hurry up. They ignored him. "You need to know… the Meghan thing… she showed up at my house and barged her way in, and I-"

Peyton covered his mouth with her hand. "I know. I didn't really think you could like someone like her. She's mean, a bully, and you are the nicest guy I've ever known."

"Nice, huh?" He smiled against her fingers. "Sounds boring."

Peyton shook her head. "Nope. Not for this girl. Nice is perfect. I don't know about you, but I'm done thinking about the past, Cam." She looped her arms around his neck. "Let's just focus on the here and now."

"I'm entirely focused on those beautiful lips of yours." His hand moved to cup her cheek, the pad of his thumb trailing across her lower lip.

Peyton, ever the impatient one, pressed her lips to his. Tilting her head back, she stepped into his embrace, relishing every moment of his kiss. With his hand splayed across her back and the other tangled in her hair, Peyton felt just right. They fit together so easily. In his arms, she wasn't too big, or not good enough. In his arms, she was just Peyton, and he was just Cam, and all those labels others used to define them didn't matter. They never mattered.

# Chapter Twenty-Two
## CAMERON

~ Cam,
   We are perfect.
   Peyton ~

Cam smiled as he let his eyes drift around the bonfire party. There weren't a lot of people there, but Peyton had only ever needed a few friends. She stood at the edge of the group talking to Addison of all people. Cam didn't know why Addie had come, but he trusted Peyton to take care of herself.

He wasn't the only one watching the pair. Julian stood near them like a bodyguard or an eavesdropper. Cam wasn't really sure which. At first, he'd thought Julian was protecting his sister from one of the school's mean girls, but the longer he watched him, the more he saw it. Julian's eyes weren't on

Peyton. He'd focused them on Addison with a mixture of longing and worry in their depths.

*Interesting.*

Cam moved on, skimming his gaze over Peyton's parents who carried the plaque she'd won, showing it to all of their friends with matching grins. It was nice to see the Callahans happy. They stood with Cam's parents. Cam watched the stiffness with which his parents interacted with the Callahans. They'd never made an effort to know the family who had become a second family to Cam. It surprised Cam when they showed up. Despite the discomfort they displayed, the fact remained. They'd come.

Cam walked around the house to where he'd parked his car on the street, stopping as he came face to face with Avery.

Dusk had fallen, but there was still enough light to make out his old friend's hardened features.

Avery stuck his hands in his pockets and rocked back on his heels as he gazed up at the house he'd once spent most of his time in.

He didn't speak, but he had to know Cam was there.

There was still so much unsaid crap between them, but that night, Cam didn't want any of it to matter. He approached Avery. "You coming around back to the bonfire?"

Avery blew out a breath. "When Mrs. Callahan invited me, I said no." He dropped his eyes to Cam. "I didn't think I could set foot in this house, that yard where we played football and had parties."

"But you're here."

Avery's eyes drifted to the house again. "I was in my car and didn't realize where I was going until I got here." He paused for a moment. "Did...did Peyton win?"

Cam nodded. "Yeah. How did you know about that?"

"The school posted online this morning about her being a finalist."

"So, everyone knows? About the app?"

He nodded, running a hand through his unkempt hair. "It's good. That she won." He scrunched his forehead. "She's…a good person. She didn't deserve what Meghan did to her."

Cam raised an eyebrow. "Avery, you've known her your entire life. App or not, she's always been a good person. Your girlfriend on the other hand… do you even like the girl you're dating?"

"I don't know." He sighed before coughing and changing the subject. "I don't think I can do this alone. Be here surrounded by the memories, I mean."

"You're not alone."

A soft voice drifted toward them as Nari appeared. "He's right." Sympathy flashed in her gaze. "You still have us, Avery. We'll walk into that yard with you."

Avery's shoulders dropped in relief, but he shook his head at the same time. "Okay. But this doesn't mean we're friends."

Nari laughed again, sarcasm entering her tone. "Of course not. You're a jock. I'm a nerd. We aren't allowed to be friends."

"Again with the labels?" Cam lifted a brow. "That's not why we're not friends, and you know it." He lifted one shoulder in a shrug. "It's because of Avery's big mouth. He's too loud for my sensitive ears."

That finally got a laugh from Avery. "I mean it. Just tonight. I'm not going to start showing up here to hang out. I have my own friends, and you guys have…things."

"Nari," Cam started. "I think Avery is saying we don't

MICHELLE MACQUEEN & ANN MAREE CRAVEN

have friends?" Ever since the award ceremony, Cam had felt lighter, more ready to smile and joke, even if it was at Avery's expense.

Nari crossed her arms. "But we have him."

"We're not—"

Cam cut Avery off. "Friends. We know. Wait here. I need to grab something from my car, and then I'll escort my non-friend into the only party he's probably ever been scared of."

As Cam walked to his car, he heard Nari behind him. "Must be a strange feeling for you, being just like any other high schooler nervous about walking into a party. Don't worry, I promise we won't make you do beer bongs or kiss anyone in closets. We know how hard it is for you just to lower yourself to hang around us. I promise our loser won't rub off on you."

Cam almost laughed at the comment. Nari said it sweetly enough, but there was the bite of honesty behind her words. She disliked Avery more than the rest of them. She'd been closer to him besides anyone other than Cooper until he decided he didn't need any of them after the accident.

Cam listened to them, preparing to play mediator. The thing about Nari, though, was she didn't fight. Honest to a fault, she was still too nice to take it further than that.

Avery stood stiffly beside her.

Cam retrieved the folder he'd brought and rejoined them. As they walked through the swampy side yard and neared the party, Avery only grew more tense.

Nari moved past her earlier comment as if it hadn't been said and talked to Avery in a low voice, soothing his nerves as best she could in her Nari way. Cam sensed he wasn't needed. He'd promised Avery he'd stay by him, but Nari held Avery's full focus. Cam suppressed a smile and left them to go find Peyton. She stood near the flames, the orange glow flickering across her face, giving her an ethereal look. Every time he saw her, she stole the breath from his lungs.

He couldn't quite believe everything that had happened that day. He'd woken up with the knowledge that she wasn't speaking to him, yet not knowing how to get her to trust him again. It turned out, all she'd needed was honesty.

He slid his arms around her from behind, reveling in how well she fit him. How was it possible that he was the one who got to touch her, kiss her? Even after everything he'd been through, he didn't feel as if he deserved her, but he'd work to change that. If there was one thing Peyton and her app taught him, it was that he deserved whatever he chose he deserved. He was worthy. If he wanted others to stop seeing him in a poor light, he had to make the first step.

He wasn't the dreaded D word. Disability didn't define him. He wasn't quite sure what defined him yet, but it wasn't some stupid label. And no one else would see that if he didn't see it himself.

Peyton leaned back into him. "Is this real?"

He smiled. She'd asked the same question the first time he kissed her almost two years ago in that tree house. "Yes, Peyton. It's real."

"You're still my best friend. You know that, right? This doesn't change anything."

He turned her in his arms. "This changes everything." He leaned in. "Sorry it took me so long." He pressed his lips to hers, and unlike the last time those exact words were spoken, he wasn't going to stop. Ever.

She pulled away to catch her breath, and her eyes fell to the folder in Cam's hand. "What's that?"

Cam stepped away from her and glanced down at his hands. "Uh…this feels so stupid now."

"Cam." She took the folder from him and flipped it open.

He shifted nervously from foot to foot.

She lifted her gaze to meet his. "What are these?"

He rubbed the back of his neck. "The emails. I printed them. Every single one. You only saw a handful posted around school, but you deserve to know everything I wanted to say to you. Some of it is pretty ugly, but I don't want to keep anything more from you."

"How many are there?" Her voice shook.

"Five hundred forty."

Her mouth fell open. "But I only sent emails for the first year. I stopped, Cam."

"I didn't. When your emails stopped coming, I kept writing. Every day." He met her heated gaze.

"You…" She shook her head, dazed. "And you want me to read them?"

"I was going through a lot, Pey. But it all led me here. You deserve to see. I want you to know all of me."

Peyton closed the folder. Before he could stop her, she tossed it into the flames. The paper folder caught fire, curling in at the edges.

Cam wanted to lunge for it. This was his big gesture. His moment to show her how far he'd come. He didn't realize he'd still been staring into the flames until Peyton slid her hands into his.

"I do know all of you, Cam."

He turned to her. "You—"

"Nothing in those emails will tell me anything new."

He pulled her against him. "I love you."

She smiled and lifted her face to his. "Good."

"Good?"

"Did you make it through all the notes from my box?"

His brow creased. "How did you know—" He shook his head. "Nari."

"You didn't answer my question."

He flashed her a sheepish smile, suddenly embarrassed she knew he'd been reading her words so often. He couldn't count how many notes he'd already made it through, but he knew how many were left. Reaching into his pocket, he pulled out one final slip of paper. He'd been carrying it around, hesitant about reading it. It wasn't that he was nervous, but he knew as soon as the words sank into his mind... "I didn't want them to be over. Pey, you wrote these notes almost two years ago when things were different, yet they've felt like everything I've needed to hear recently, like you were showing me who I was, who I thought I'd lost."

Her answering smile warmed him from the inside out. She slid the paper from his hand and unfolded it. He'd imagined her voice each time he read one of her notes, but here, now, she was finally in front of him.

"You're not perfect." She stifled a laugh.

"Gee, thanks."

"Hush, you." She pressed a hand across his mouth so she could keep reading. "But us, we are perfect. I may be outing myself here and setting myself up for a world of pain, but some day, I hope you see it to."

Cam stuck his tongue out, licking her hand that still covered his mouth. She ripped it back with a shriek. "Ew, Cam!"

He caught her around the waist before she could widen the space between them. "No world of pain. I promise."

Red tinged her cheeks. "The girl who wrote those notes

MICHELLE MACQUEEN & ANN MAREE CRAVEN

knew she'd never be good enough for you. She didn't think she was pretty enough, worthy enough. But she also never thought you'd actually read all the notes."

"Pey." He put his fingers under her chin and tilted her head back. "You're the most beautiful thing I've ever seen." Cam wrapped an arm around her shoulders. "I do have a confession to make."

"I'm listening. Cam confessions are my favorite."

He chuckled. "Well, you see, you were wrong."

"When?" A defensive tone entered her voice as if she could never be wrong about something. It only made him laugh more.

"Your first note to me. It said 'Above all, you love to run.'"

"And?" She chewed on her lower lip.

"I enjoyed running, but I always loved you more. Even when I was a kid and my feelings were solely about friendship, it was you, not running, that pushed me toward my goals. Running is only a sport, a competition. Maybe all this time, I was only running to get to you."

She released her lip. "Man, you're cheesy."

He raised a brow. "The only question is, does cheesy work for you?"

"Hell yes." She rose up on her toes, claiming his lips with hers.

He pulled her body flush against his. For a blissful moment, everything else disappeared. There were no old friends struggling to find each other again. There was no robot leg, no crushing pain of loss. Theirs was a world inhabited by two people who'd rid themselves of every ounce of self-doubt.

It didn't matter what anyone thought of them. Not anymore.

A few whistles broke them apart, and the real world crashed down on Cam. Pain shot up Cam's leg, telling him he needed to sit down, but he couldn't. Not yet. Not when Peyton felt so right in his arms.

Julian and his dad catcalled toward them. Nari whistled again. Cam's parents wore matching pleased expressions.

Mrs. Callahan walked toward them. "About time." She smiled and wrapped an arm around each of them, breaking them apart and leading them away from the fire. "Now, let's talk about some ground rules. We all love you, Cameron, but I'm far too young to be a grandma."

"Mom!" Peyton screeched.

Cam laughed before covering it up with a cough, his face turning serious. "Of course. I know what protection is for."

"Cameron!" Peyton covered her eyes and shrugged away from her mom. "I hate you both."

"No, you don't," Cam called as Peyton rushed away, taking refuge with Nari. "You love me. No take backs!"

She shot him a smile over her shoulder, a true, honest to God smile. The kind he used to wish she reserved only for him. But bottling up her joy would be like clipping a bird's wings, holding it back when it was meant to fly.

And more than anything, he wanted to help her soar.

# Chapter Twenty-Three

## CAMERON

~ Cam,

*Some day, I hope you see it too.*

*Peyton ~*

Cam couldn't continue to dwell on the accident. Almost two years had passed, and it was time to move on. They wouldn't move on from Cooper—he'd forever be a part of them—but living in the past only brought pain. He'd once thought his future had been taken from him with his leg, that he'd never be the same. He hadn't known then that his injury changed nothing. He was still the same boy he'd always been with big dreams.

The dreams had changed. He would no longer run—at least competitively. He'd probably never be able to give it up entirely, no matter how uncomfortable it was.

Peyton sat on the front stoop of her house when he pulled up. A soft white fleece was wrapped around her shoulders to protect her from the autumn wind. She'd pulled her long hair back away from her face, giving him a clear view of peachy skin and wide eyes.

His heart stuttered as he shut off the engine.

She got to her feet and skipped across the expansive lawn, throwing her arms around him. "Cam," she breathed. "I missed you."

He chuckled, the sound muffled in her shoulder. "It's only been a few hours."

They'd stayed up late the night before, making up for lost time. He wanted to kiss her for hours, so he had, never tiring of her lips or the breathy sounds she made.

They'd moved past any weirdness they felt about kissing after being friends for so long and had spent the past week wrapped around each other. At school, most of their peers had gone back to ignoring both of them. It was strange to return to normal life after something so monumental happened.

No one else cared that two teenagers had professed their love for one another. They were just another couple, faceless nobodies in a sea of people trying to get through high school.

If they'd had any illusions about their old group of friends reuniting, they were broken as soon as school began that next Monday. Nari sat with Cam and Peyton at lunch, but Avery and Addison acted as if nothing had changed. Occasionally, Cam would catch one of them watching him and Peyton across the lunch room. He'd give a small wave and then return to the friends who were in front of him.

Julian was another matter. Cam rarely saw him grace the

halls of Twin Rivers High. He'd gotten rid of the surly attitude, though. At least around Cam.

Cam opened the car door for Peyton. As she slid in, another car pulled up behind him. Nari got out and froze as she realized he was there.

"Cam." Her eyes widened.

He flashed her a smile. "Hey! You here to see Pey? We're heading to the river."

She flicked her eyes to the front door where Julian had appeared. "Um, no. I can't. Sorry."

Cam shrugged. "Okay. Catch you later."

"Later."

Cam climbed into his BMW and pulled onto the street. As they drove away, he saw Nari in the rearview mirror pulling a bag from her car. He didn't know what was going on, but she'd tell them, eventually.

Peyton twisted in her seat, watching Nari and Julian until the car rounded the corner.

"I'm sure everything is fine." Cam reached across the center console and took her hand.

She relaxed in her seat.

They parked near the one place Cam had yet to go. He'd visited the falls many times and driven over the bridge, but he hadn't stopped at the place where it happened, where the car spun across the bridge on ice before plunging into the water.

Peyton hadn't asked any questions when Cam asked her to come with him. She hadn't said anything about it at all, and he'd been grateful.

"Can I..." He cleared his throat. "Can I have a minute?"

"Of course." She leaned toward him, her lips grazing his cheek. "Take all the time you need."

He brushed the bangs from her forehead and stared at her for a long moment, letting her give him the courage. Sucking in a deep breath, he got out of the car.

A few cars drove across the bridge in either direction. It wasn't usually a busy road, but it was the only way to get to the other side of town.

Two years ago, there'd been only a small metal rail dividing the bridge from the drop off into the water. Now, a wall of concrete had been erected on each side. Signs telling drivers to be careful stood where none had before.

Would it have helped? Probably not.

A narrow sidewalk sat between the road and the concrete wall going across the bridge. Cam took the path until he reached the midway point. He could still hear it. Crunching metal. Squealing tires. The unstable car hadn't plunged off the edge right away. It had hung suspended, rocking back and forth before tipping over.

It wasn't a far drop to the water, but it had been enough.

A car whipped by, and Cam felt the wind on his face before peace set in. He'd never felt at peace about the accident. It had taken him a long time to stand there without the crushing weight of guilt and sadness clouding his mind.

"Hey, Coop." He smiled, wondering how it all worked. Was Cooper still around? Did he watch them, listening when his name came up?

Or was he just...gone?

"I still don't know everything that happened that night." He ran a hand over the rough surface of the wall. "I had to come. To stand in the place where everything changed." He breathed out slowly. "Julian is keeping something about that party from us, but I think it's okay. I think maybe I don't want to know. You're gone, buddy, but I'm still here. It's taken me too long to see that. I'm sorry I've taken it for granted."

He glanced toward the end of the bridge where Peyton leaned against his car watching him.

A smile curved his lips. "You'd kick my butt for the thoughts I have about your sister." He chuckled. "I know you loved her. You loved Julian too in your own way." He gestured for Peyton to join him.

"I'm going to prove to her just how beautiful she is every day for the rest of my life. Inside and out. That's my promise to you, Coop."

Peyton joined him, sliding her arms around his waist.

He sighed in contentment. "We're going to miss you forever, man."

Peyton rested her chin on his shoulder, her eyes glassy. "I love you, brother."

Cam kissed the top of her head. "I'm sorry for everything that had to happen to bring us here." Those words were for Peyton, not Coop.

She lifted her tear-stained face to peer up at him. "Don't you dare start with the guilt, Cameron Tucker. None of this happened because of that stupid accident. Remember that night?"

How could he forget?

"We were going to do this whether tragedy hit us or not. If anything, the accident made it take us longer."

He held her tighter. "I wasn't feeling guilty."

Her lips pursed as if she didn't believe him.

"Scouts honor."

"You were never a scout."

He grinned. "Fine, but I'm telling the truth. No guilt. I'm...happy."

"You say that like it's the most incredulous word that's ever left your lips."

He shrugged and looked to the sky once more. "Close your eyes, Coop."

Peyton yelped in surprise as Cam dipped her back, plastering his lips to hers. She laughed when he finally pulled her up.

"You think Coop would have approved of that?" Cam pulled Peyton's ponytail, and she swatted his hand away.

"Oh, totally." Her lips stretched into a smile. "He loved us both. We can miss him, but he wouldn't want us to let that control our lives."

Cam pulled Peyton back toward the car. "Come on. It's Saturday. Let's make a deal. The past can't haunt us anymore. Who knows what the future holds? But, right now, Peyton Callahan, well, right now, I just want to enjoy the moment with the girl who makes every moment worth it."

She suppressed her grin, muttering under her breath. "Cheesy."

They reached the car, and he spun her around, pressing her against the passenger door. "Good, I think you like me cheesy."

She ran a finger over his bottom lip. "Cameron, I like you any way I can have you."

He pressed a quick kiss to her lips before pulling her aside and opening the door. "Vamonos. We have so much to do together."

She got into the car and shut the door. Cam ran to the other side and slid in.

"I know you, Cam. How many of these things involve our lips?" Peyton crossed her arms in mock admonishment.

Cam shot her a wink before starting the engine and

pulling away. He watched the bridge disappear in the rearview mirror. "Bye, Coop."

They'd never escape from the memories in Twin Rivers, but as time went on, they didn't have to hurt so much. Cam once thought leaving town, leaving the place where everything changed, would help him move on. But that was the thing with fear and pain. It magnified the more you try to hide from it.

The only true way to rid yourself of the past is to face it head-on, to stare it down until it no longer stared back at you.

A smile slid across Cam's face. He'd finally fought the battle.

And he'd won.

He'd won everything.

# Epilogue

## NARI

Nari stood in Addison's driveway watching the snow flurry around her. The expansive property ran all the way to the edge of the river. If you squinted, you could even see Defiance Falls with its roaring waters and the Defiance bridge in the distance. Back in the house, the party continued on as if the boys had never been there at all. She wasn't sure why Julian and Cooper had been at each other's throats this time, only that Peyton was right to throw her own brothers out. Cam and Avery were a packaged deal with Coop. As much as Nari wanted Cam to stay, to finally figure out what he and Peyton were, she knew he wouldn't abandon his friends. Especially when Avery was so drunk.

Coop had a few drinks as well, but he was better at hiding his inebriation. He'd had plenty of practice.

Nari wrapped her arms around herself as the cold wound up through the sleeves of her fleece jacket. A flake landed on her lips and melted under her hot breath. She hated parties, never quite feeling as if she belonged.

*Addison invited the cheerleading squad, and the football team followed them like a pack of rabid dogs. Addie would be pleased, but sometimes, Nari didn't know how they were all friends. Peyton, she understood. Both outcasts, they had a lot in common. But Addison was a cheerleader, Coop and Avery both ruled the football field, Cam was destined for the Olympic track team, and Julian... was the loner always on the edge of the group but never quite part of it.*

*They were an odd bunch.*

*She turned to retreat to Addison's house, the promise of warmth winning out over a desire to be alone. Out of the corner of her eye, she caught headlights coming to a halt on the bridge in the distance. A second car joined it.*

*Nari took off running across the snowy lawn, stopping as she made out the horrific scene. She couldn't see any people, but the shadow of a car hung over the edge of the bridge, threatening to plunge into the icy current below.*

*She pulled her gloves off and fumbled her phone from her pocket, dialing three numbers she hoped would help.*

*"9-1-1," the operator answered. "What's your emergency?"*

Nari leaned her head on the lunch table, her eyes sliding shut. She'd had the dream again. The one where she was an unknown bystander in a stranger's crash. It wasn't the first time. Only, maybe it wasn't a dream, but simply a memory. They hadn't been strangers, though she didn't know that at the time.

In her panicked brain, she'd never once considered the passengers hanging precariously off the bridge had been her friends. She didn't yet know how that night, that crash, was going to change them forever.

"Nari." Peyton's voice reached her.

Nari lifted her eyes, not bothering to raise her head. "Hey."

Peyton's brow crinkled with worry. "I've been trying to get your attention for the past minute."

Nari yawned. "Sorry. I'm just tired."

Peyton's lips drew down. "Are you sleeping?"

"Yes, Mother." It wasn't a lie. Nari could fall asleep easy enough, but some nights the dream would come back. She couldn't say that though. She'd never told anyone she was the one to call in the accident. She should have done more. Cooper died and Cameron lost his leg. Part of her couldn't help but think if she'd known it was them on the bridge... No, she couldn't let herself go down that rabbit hole. Not again.

"Nari." Peyton shook her head. "Maybe you should go home."

Nari closed her eyes again. She couldn't afford to miss any school. When her dreams weren't causing a fitful sleep, it was her anxiety over the grades she couldn't seem to raise. "You know my mom would never allow that."

With a sigh, she lifted her head from the table, removed her glasses, and scrubbed a hand over her face. If she were honest with herself, she preferred being at school than at home. There were fewer expectations here. People took one look at her and assumed they knew her and never questioned their perceptions.

Setting her thick-framed glasses back on her nose, she dug in to the lunch her mom sent her with. For years, she'd begged to be allowed to buy lunch at school rather than enduring the strange looks for being a senior still carrying a rainbow lunchbox.

Peyton smiled when Nari set the box on the table. "I'm sorry, I just love that thing. It's so you."

Nari only shrugged. If it wasn't for their judgmental classmates, maybe she'd like it too. She pulled out a seaweed wrap filled with egg and vegetables, eyeing Peyton's pizza longingly as she did. Mondays were always pizza day, and she envied the kids in the long line waiting for their greasy goodness.

Peyton looked down at her tray. "Ugh, I don't know if I can stomach all this grease."

Most people probably assumed Peyton dieted because she wasn't rail thin like the cheerleaders, but Nari knew the truth. She just preferred healthy food.

With a grin, Nari slid her wrap toward Peyton and swapped it with Peyton's pizza. Peyton's eyes lit up, and Nari laughed. "You could have just asked. You know I'll never turn down anything slathered in so much cheese."

Peyton raised a brow. "Your mother would have a heart attack seeing that."

Nari responded with a closed-mouth grin, her mouth full of deliciousness.

"I don't know how you're so tiny."

Nari shrugged. "Probably because I'm Asian."

Peyton choked on her next bite.

"You talking about Asians without me?" Cam dropped his tray onto the table and sat beside Peyton, kissing her cheek as he did. If Nari didn't like them so much, she'd have been sickened by their sweetness.

She swallowed her bite and reached for her water bottle, taking a swig. "Just that all the Korean t'aekwŏndo I do burns a lot of calories. You know, the typical stereotype stuff."

Cam nodded. "I knew it. Every stereotype we've ever heard is true."

Nari shrugged. "It's what Hollywood demands of us. We Korean Americans have to conform to what they want to portray in their movies. We practice martial arts while singing K-Pop in front of our screaming fans and doing our super brainy math homework all at the same time." She couldn't hold her serious expression anymore, her face splitting into a grin. She loved her friends. As the only Korean American at Twin Rivers High, she stood out. People expected things of her that were nothing more than a stereotype. Even popular kids she never spoke to sometimes asked her to tutor them in math or science.

She'd laughed in more than a few faces. She might be nerd-like—their word, not hers—but she'd be no use to anyone as a tutor.

Cam and Peyton never expected her to be anyone other than herself.

Cam dug in to his pizza, shaking his head. He pointed his slice at her. "The Korean martial artist and the robot. Sounds like a great movie."

He started calling himself a robot since revealing his artificial leg to his friends. In the accident that took Cooper's life, Cameron went over the falls with a badly broken leg. He managed to get himself out of the river, but he passed out more than a mile from the accident. After a night out in the elements, infection set in, and amputation ultimately saved his life. But then he left town. It wasn't until he returned eighteen months later that they learned what the accident really cost him.

MICHELLE MACQUEEN & ANN MAREE CRAVEN

Feeling more energized with some food in her and the joking with her friends, Nari scanned the lunchroom. People talked behind whispered hands, their eyes bouncing between a single table and the phones they held in front of them.

Nari saw the video over the weekend. Avery St. Germaine lost Twin Rivers High the playoffs with an epic bonehead play. It looked as if he'd forgotten what team he played for when he threw the ball to the wrong player and lost the game.

The man in question sat at the same table he did every day, his shoulders hunched forward. She watched him for a few moments, noting how none of his *friends* even spoke to him. Meghan, the girl he'd apparently dumped over the weekend, sat at the other end draped over one of his teammates.

Someone ruffled Nari's hair as they walked by. She pushed the dark strands out of her eyes, looking up in time to catch Beckett's wink before he slid into the empty seat beside Avery, slapping him on the back.

"Earth to Nari." Peyton didn't sound annoyed, only amused.

Cam chuckled to himself. "Since when are you friends with Becks Anderson?"

She shrugged.

"Oh my gosh, Nari." Peyton grabbed her arm. "Are you into Beckett?"

She couldn't stop the laugh from bursting past her lips. Beckett? What would they say if they knew she spent her weekends singing on stage beside him? No, she didn't like Becks Anderson. Not like that. They were from different worlds. Plus, he was more like a brother.

Her eyes drifted back to Avery. At least Becks talked to

218

him. She watched Avery shake his head and stand before storming from the lunchroom.

Nari sighed. She'd been on the receiving end of her fair share of judgment at their school. Avery was just another one of the kids who made others feel unwelcome, unwanted. So, why did her gut twist in sympathy for him? Avery was nothing more than her jerk neighbor, someone she'd once considered a close friend.

A few kids sitting at the other end of Nari's table giggled over their phones. She heard the telltale sound of the announcers.

"He ruined the entire season on that play," an underclassman she didn't know said.

"Yeah," another agreed. "He deserves everything he gets today."

The accident came back to Nari. Avery had been in that car and could have died if Julian and Cam hadn't been there to help him back to shore. Maybe that was why she'd always felt protective of him. He tried to act as if nothing bothered him, but she saw through the bravado.

She pushed her chair back and stood, gathering her trash into her lunchbox. Before she could second-guess herself, she turned to the underclassman.

"Do you really think a high school football game matters? Everyone knows Avery St. Germaine has already received dozens of offers from high-profile colleges. This will be old news by next week. But you, you'll never get over your petty bullcrap." She hadn't realized she'd raised her voice until the surrounding tables went quiet. Someone laughed, and she knew it was probably over the term bullcrap. Her classmates used to make a game out of trying to get her to swear, but it just wasn't her.

Beckett met her eyes curiously, but no one else dared.

Nari swept a scowl around the room. "Don't we all have a hard enough time without shining a spotlight on every stupid mistake we make? Last month, it was Peyton's ripped pants, and now this?"

"Yeah, let's not bring that back around," Peyton whisper-shouted.

Shock flashed across many of the faces. *That's right. Nari Won Song, quiet nerd girl is sick and tired of the way people are treated at Twin Rivers High.* She knew the minute she walked out of that cavernous room Avery would no longer be the subject of their conversations.

After doing her best to stay in the shadows for almost four years, Nari had stepped into the spotlight.

Nausea swirled through her, and her confidence swept away on the current of whispers. She yanked her lunch box from the table and ran from the lunchroom, finding peace in the blissfully quiet hall.

Peyton would look for her. She'd worry. But Nari didn't have the capacity to think of that when her pulse pounded in her head. What had she just done?

Creeping through the empty halls, she went to the one place she could be sure to hide from the brain-dead idiots of her school.

The library.

Nari might have trouble with most of her classes, but when it came to books, she couldn't get enough. She stepped through the doors into her sanctuary. Mrs. Laurel looked up, giving Nari a knowing smile.

As Nari expected, few students meandered through the stacks. A couple sat at the row of computers along the far wall by the large windows looking out on the football field.

The sight only reminded her of her little speech in the lunch-room, and her cheeks heated.

Why had she done it? She couldn't take it back though she wasn't sure she wished she could. Each word was true. Twin Rivers High had a problem. Every perceived flaw was outed by their classmates. It was like a jungle, divided by predators and their prey. The strong ate the weak.

And Nari had always been one of the weak.

Needing something to take her mind off what happened and to shake the exhaustion from her body, she ducked behind a tall shelf. Her fingers skimmed the spines of the books until she came to her favorite author. David Eddings wrote tales of magic and adventure, stories she could lose herself in.

As she pulled a book free, someone slammed into her, gripping her arms to keep her from falling.

"Sorry," he grumbled.

Nari lifted her eyes to find Avery staring down at her, dark circles under his eyes. He ran a hand through his chestnut hair, messing it up more than it already was. They tried to step around each other at the same time and just ended up colliding again.

"Nari." He sighed, placing his large hands on her shoulders to hold her in place as he moved around her.

Pity tugged at her, and she knew he'd hate it. But it wasn't like she couldn't help her feelings. "I didn't know you knew where the library was." It was meant to be a joke, and Nari winced when it came out sounding more like a condemnation.

Avery's brows tugged together. "We can't all be geniuses like you, nerd."

He called her nerd even when they were friends, but

back then, he said it with a great deal of affection. Now, it only felt like a label he stuck across her forehead like everyone else. She crossed her arms. "Oh, right, you have better things to do like messing up football plays." She hated herself for the words as soon as they crossed her lips. In recent years, Avery brought out the worst in her. She didn't know why.

He tensed. "Yeah, okay." He lowered his head and walked away.

Nari turned, following him with her eyes. "Avery, wait." He didn't stop, so she jogged to his side, and they rounded the corner into a new row of books. "I'm sorry."

This row dead-ended into a concrete wall. Avery reached it and stopped when his phone dinged in his pocket. Pulling it free, he pressed his thumb against it to unlock the screen. Muttering a curse under his breath, he dropped down to sit with his back against the wall.

Nari twisted the fingers of her free hand in the hem of her yellow shirt, curling the others around the handle of her lunch box. "Are you okay?"

He threw his phone with another curse, and it skittered across the floor.

"I'm going to take that as a no." She leaned over to pick up his phone. The screen showed a picture obviously taken at lunch. Meghan sat in the lap of Andrew Bradley, broad-shouldered fullback of the football team. Their faces were plastered together in a kiss. The caption read "Are you going to let her show you up like this?"

Nari glanced behind her, wondering if it was time to make her escape. She wasn't the person Avery needed right now, but there was no one else. Releasing a breath, she sat on the ground facing him and held out his phone.

He took it, his fingers grazing hers for a fraction of a second.

"You can go." He refused to look at her.

"I know." She rested her arms on her legs. "I thought you broke up with her."

Finally meeting her gaze, he shrugged. "I did."

"Well, whoever sent that to you obviously thought it would bother you."

"Everything bothers me today."

"Do I?"

"Yes." He didn't even hesitate. Nari knew one of the reasons Avery didn't like her. She knew more about his life than anyone at school. He was revered as the son of an NFL player. His team followed his lead because of it. They didn't hear his father screaming drunk every night. They'd never overheard his mom telling theirs of money problems. Although, she was pretty sure Avery didn't know about those problems either.

She stayed silent for a long moment, letting him think. He fiddled on his phone, his eyes going wide as he started a video one of his friends sent him. Nari froze when she heard her own voice. The video was of her rant only minutes ago.

Avery lifted his eyes to hers. "Why would you defend me? I'm a jerk."

"Yes." She huffed. "You are. And you've never had to live as the butt of your stupid clique's jokes before. I have. My friends have. I didn't do that for you."

That was only partially true. She'd felt sorry for him, but in that moment, she was also angry.

"Good," he grunted. "I don't want to owe you anything." Something sparked in his eyes. "Wait, I have an idea."

She groaned. "That sentence is how the world ends. With

Avery St. Germaine actually having an original idea. Then we all explode."

To her surprise, he laughed. A true, body-shaking laugh.

She raised a brow. "Go on. Tell me this brilliant idea."

"Kiss me."

Now it was her turn to laugh. "See? I knew the world was ending."

"No, hear me out. If I send my friends a picture of you and me, it'll get back to Meghan. After your little display at lunch, they'll all believe it, and it would get them off my back."

Nari got to her feet. "You're delusional. I wouldn't kiss you if I was dying and you were the only cure."

He stood to face her. "That's a little extreme."

"I'm an extreme person."

"Oh, I remember exactly who you are, Nari Won Song."

She hated that he knew her so well. They'd been friends for too long, but that was in the past. For two years now, he'd done nothing but cause all their friends pain. He'd become one of the people they once vowed never to be.

Shoving her glasses up her nose, Nari turned.

"Please." Avery sounded so pathetic, but the idea was ridiculous.

"I'm not going to let you use me to make your ex jealous. If you know me so well, you should have known not to ask." She started walking away.

"I just thought you'd want to help me like old times, Nari."

"We're not friends, Avery. You've said it yourself. Many times." She shook her head at the insanity of his suggestion.

Kiss Avery? She wasn't about to admit to the king of the jocks that she'd never kissed anyone before. At eighteen, she was a kissing virgin. But Avery St. Germaine was not going to be her first. She had better sense than that. She didn't look back at him again as she made her way out of the library.

The bell rang, signaling the end of lunch period. As Nari opened her locker and stuffed her lunch box inside, she realized she wasn't tired anymore. The hilarious conversation with Avery energized her. She pulled out her pre-calculus book and slammed her locker, preparing herself for an hour of complete and utter torture. Despite her abysmal math grades, Nari's parents insisted she take all the top math courses offered at Twin Rivers High.

Sliding behind her desk at the back of the classroom, she watched Avery enter the room, joining his friends at the far end as if they hadn't spent the entire lunch period ignoring him. She shook her head. How could they treat each other so poorly and then act like they were okay?

Avery didn't glance back at Nari once, and she didn't know if she was grateful for his usual aloofness or annoyed that she once again ceased to exist.

Want to find out if Nari could be just what Avery needs? You can see their story in Nerdy Girls Can Rock! Available wherever you buy books.

**Want two free Curvy Girls can Rule prequels? Find out what happened the night of the accident by joining up to receive updates from us at**
https://michellelynnauthor.com/joinus

# What's Next?

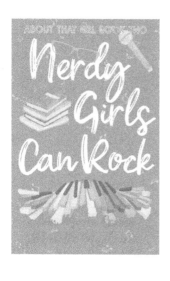

**Neighbors aren't supposed to fake a relationship.**

**They're also not supposed to kiss like it's real** Eighteen months ago, an accident didn't only take their friend, it took their friendship too.

Nari can't remember the last time she spoke with Avery, the last time she thought of him without anger. He's mean, cruel, he sits atop the food chain at school, looking down on nerds like her.

Nari is a nerd in looks only. When falling grades set her back, Avery proposes a deal. Pretend to be his girlfriend to get back at his ex, and he'll make sure she passes math.

It sounds easy enough, and there's little risk. She's too focused on sinking grades and the rock band no one can know about to fall for the boy next door.

But this boy next door... well, he might just fall for her.

**Available now**

# About Michelle

Michelle MacQueen is a USA Today bestselling author of love. Yes, love. Whether it be YA romance, NA romance, or fantasy romance (Under M. Lynn), she loves to make readers swoon.

The great loves of her life to this point are two tiny blond creatures who call her "aunt" and proclaim her books to be "boring books" for their lack of pictures. Yet, somehow, she still manages to love them more than chocolate.

When she's not sharing her inexhaustible wisdom with her niece and nephew, Michelle is usually lounging in her ridiculously large bean bag chair creating worlds and characters that remind her to smile every day - even when a feisty five-year-old is telling her just how much she doesn't know.

**Want to see more books by Michelle? Visit Books2Read.com to shop a complete list of her works**

# About Ann Maree

 Ann Maree Craven is an Amazon best-selling author of Young Adult Contemporary Fiction and YA Fantasy (her Fantasy fans will know her as Melissa A. Craven). Her books focus on strong female protagonists who aren't always perfect, but they find their inner strength along the way. She believes in stories that make you think and she loves playing with foreshadowing, leaving clues and hints for the careful reader.

Ann Maree draws inspiration from her background in interior design to help her with the small details in world building and scene settings. She is a diehard introvert with a wicked sense of humor and a tendency for hermit-like behavior. (Seriously, she gets cranky if she has to put on anything other than yoga pants and t-shirts!)

Her favorite pastime is sitting on her porch when the weather is nice with her two dogs, Fynlee and Nahla, reading from her massive TBR pile and dreaming up new stories.

Visit Melissaacraven.com for more information about the series and discover exclusive content.

**Want to see more books by Ann Maree? Visit Books2Read.com to shop a complete list of her works**